P9-DDB-830

Gentle's Holler

PRAISE FOR *Gentle's Holler:*

"Kerry Madden, like her heroine Livy Two, has a rare gift for words. From page one she makes the reader care deeply about this warm and compelling mountain family. The book is rich in detail about their simple pleasures and their trials. I loved the family and the book."
∞ Betsy Byars, Newbery Medal–winning author of *The Summer of the Swans*

"Although spiked with sad and even tragic times, this book is filled with the kind of characters we all fall in love with, and the story glows with warm and tender feelings that are ultimately what we all hope to instill in our children." ∞ Audrey Couloumbis, Newbery Honor–winning author of *Getting Near to Baby*

"Visit *Gentle's Holler* in the company of twelve-year-old aspiring songwriter Livy Two Weems, and you won't ever want to leave. Both heartfelt and heartbreaking, *Gentle's Holler* is a story of music, mountains, and the everyday magic of love. It's a story that's rich and true, and Livy Two, Gentle, Uncle Hazard, and the rest of the rambunctious Weems clan will stay with you long after you turn the last page."
∞ Jennifer Donnelly, Printz Honor–winning author of *A Northern Light*

"Country life is as unfamiliar to me as life on Mars, but with Livy Two as my guide, I found it fascinating. I trusted her completely. And I would have happily followed her anywhere. I envy anyone who has yet to meet her for the first time." ∞ Amy Goldman Koss, author of *The Girls*

"This book is the genuine article. Its lively humor and mountain poverty are married flawlessly. Its heroine, Livy Two, is as bone-real and as endearing as Kate DiCamillo's Opal in *Because of Winn-Dixie*."
∞ Rosemary Wells, author of *Mary on Horseback*

Gentle's Holler

A NOVEL

~ BY ~

KERRY MADDEN

VIKING

VIKING
Published by Penguin Group
Penguin Young Readers Group, 345 Hudson Street, New York, New York 10014, U.S.A.
Penguin Group (Canada), 90 Eglinton Avenue East, Suite 700, Toronto, Ontario, Canada M4P 2Y3
(a division of Pearson Penguin Canada Inc.)
Penguin Books Ltd, 80 Strand, London WC2R 0RL, England
Penguin Ireland, 25 St Stephen's Green, Dublin 2, Ireland (a division of Penguin Books Ltd)
Penguin Group (Australia), 250 Camberwell Road, Camberwell, Victoria 3124, Australia
(a division of Pearson Australia Group Pty Ltd)
Penguin Books India Pvt Ltd, 11 Community Centre, Panchsheel Park, New Delhi – 110 017, India
Penguin Group (NZ), Cnr Airborne and Rosedale Roads, Albany, Auckland 1310, New Zealand
(a division of Pearson New Zealand Ltd)
Penguin Books (South Africa) (Pty) Ltd, 24 Sturdee Avenue, Rosebank,
Johannesburg 2196, South Africa

Penguin Books Ltd, Registered Offices: 80 Strand, London WC2R 0RL, England

First published in 2005 by Viking, a division of Penguin Young Readers Group

5 7 9 10 8 6

Text copyright © Kerry Madden, 2005
All rights reserved

LIBRARY OF CONGRESS CATALOGING-IN-PUBLICATION DATA
Madden, Kerry.
Gentle's Holler / by Kerry Madden.
p. cm.
Summary: In the early 1960s, twelve-year-old songwriter Livy Two Weems dreams of seeing
the world beyond the Maggie Valley, North Carolina, holler where she lives in poverty with
her parents and eight brothers and sisters, but understands that she must put family first.
ISBN 0-670-05998-6 (hardcover)
[1. Family life—North Carolina—Fiction. 2. Music—Fiction. 3. Poverty—Fiction. 4. Blind—Fiction.
5. People with disabilities—Fiction. 6. North Carolina—History—20th century—Fiction.] I. Title.
PZ7.M2555Ge 2005
[Fic]—dc22
2004018424

Printed in U.S.A.
Set in Granjon
Book design by Kelley McIntyre

For Inge, who taught Norah, Lucy,
and Flannery at Eagle Rock Montessori,
and who offered her garden as a writing place

And for Kiffen,
who taught me about gardens, constellations,
and the ballads of Appalachia

And for Mama Frances and her thirteen children:
Beanie, Jim, Nancy, Tomi, Teresa, Celina,
Kiffen, Joseph, Eppie, John, Chauvie,
Sam, and Silas

In memory of Renee Hahn,
who blessed generations of children in Los Angeles
with her loving, gentle hands,

∽ and ∽

Catherine Johana Garcia,
a beautiful twelve-year-old girl who loved
flowers, dolphins, and stories

~ Contents ~

Gentle's Holler

CHAPTER ONE

Daddy's Roasted Peanuts

From the high branch of our old red maple where I sit under a starry sky, I spy Mama in the bedroom tending to the babies. Down on the porch below, Daddy picks the banjo soft and sweet. Mama covers up my little sister, Gentle, who used to sleep in the shirt drawer in Mama and Daddy's bedroom. Now she shares a crib with the twins, Caroline and Cyrus, because Mama just had herself another girl child named Appelonia who claims Gentle's drawer.

I reckon in this family that's how you know you've done gone and graduated from being a baby—going from drawer to crib. Though Gentle sleeps in the granny's crib with the twins, none of them are much babies anymore. They're more like three growing snap beans, with Gentle near three and the twins already four years old. It's called a granny's crib because during the day, Mama can fold it up to look like a regular chair, and Mama says with so many folks in the house we need all the chairs we can get. At night, all the little ones sleep snaked around each other like warm puzzle pieces.

I gaze up at the sky to study the star patterns in the midnight skies, and I reckon I'm right partial to the Pleiades, the Seven Sisters, because I have seven sisters myself. I also have two brothers, one older and one younger. Of the sisters, one is dead, but I like to believe that my sister Olivia is up there in that mini-dipper winking down on us in Maggie Valley. I can only see the Pleiades for some of the year, but I know they're there all the same—just like I feel my sister Olivia close to me when I can't sleep late at night and nothing will do but to breathe in a midnight sky of summer stars.

"Livy Two! You get in here right now or I'm telling Mama!" My big sister Becksie pokes her head out the window from her own bunk bed, like to scare me half to death. Becksie's real name is Rebecca, and she is by far the bossiest creature to ever live.

"That's right," sniffs Becksie's itchy-mosquito echo, Jitters, who's all of nine. "You gonna fall out of that tree and break your neck, Livy Two, and that's the truth."

Jitters's name is Myrtle-Anne, but we call her Jitters since she's always breaking something. She don't mean to drop things or trip over her own two feet, but Mama says some kids are just born with more "jitters" and that she'll outgrow it soon enough.

"Listen," I say, "I'll be in directly, but right now, I'm praying to Livy One so you'uns hush up and leave me be."

That shuts them up quick. Can't argue with praying to a dead sister. Of course, I'm not really praying to Livy One, though I do like to talk to her sometimes, mostly about our little sister Gentle, whose eyes don't work right. My belly gets to aching when I think on Gentle's eyes, but Mama and Daddy shush me up quick if I get to asking too many questions. Most Mama will say is, "Gentle will use her eyes when she's ready, Livy Two. Now check the cornbread in the oven, little gal."

So I whisper my questions to my sister in the stars, who has given me no answers so far. Though she died at birth, Mama and Daddy didn't see no use in wasting the name, so as I was the next girl born, I became Olivia Hyatt Weems too. Livy Two for short.

Daddy says the name Olivia beholds the fragrance of sweet, creek-side magnolia blossoms. Daddy's a poet in his soul, but not Mama. She claims a paycheck is worth a sight more than a dang poem. Daddy doesn't have a regular paycheck, which worries her to death, but Daddy don't believe in worries. He says Mama worries enough for the both of them. When Mama tells Daddy that we're running low on food, Daddy says, "Darling, I swear if these children didn't have stomachs, they'd be angels." But we got stomachs, all right, and hands, and my hands are usually on the neck of a guitar that Daddy give me for my birthday last year though we couldn't hardly afford it. He said it was for all of us, but I knew he meant it for me, cause none of the other kids cared a lick about playing it. Mama says, "No more musicians in the family, thank you," but she lets me play as long as I get my chores done.

I'll be twelve years old come January, but the older I get, the more I realize how little I know about the world beyond Maggie Valley. I wonder if there are other girls like me sitting in trees after dark, wondering what the future holds. Will I ever meet these other girls? If our paths cross, will we recognize each other? They say Maggie Valley was named for a real Maggie who lived in the Smokies in the early 1900s and whose daddy ran the post office. They say this Maggie hated her name, but I like it fine. Maggie Valley sounds a peck nicer than East Flat Rock or Enka-Stinka, other places we used to live. I like living in a town named for a girl who lived in these mountains long ago with nothing but dirt roads for wagons, but I also know I want to see the world beyond the Smokies, and I aim to bring my guitar with me when I do.

One day, I'd like to stroll along the Great Wall of China, ride me a camel in Egypt, swim in the Ganges River way over in India, and sip a cup of tea with the queen of England. I also intend to take a boat to see the northern lights called the aurora borealis where folks say the lights dance on the horizon in a burst of colors. Sometimes, I get so excited thinking of all the places I got to go that I can't hardly breathe. But for now, I can only read about them far-off folks and places in the lending library truck that shows up about once a month in Maggie Valley. Still, I have seen three famous people in my life: 1) Mr. Cas Walker, who broadcasts the "Farm and Home Hour" radio show way over in Knoxville, Tennessee. 2) Mr. Roberto Clemente, a Pittsburgh Pirate and one of the best right fielders in the game of baseball, according to my brother, Emmett. We seen Mr. Clemente at an exhibition game in Greenville when we was visiting Mama's kin. 3) Miss Patsy Cline at the Buncombe County fair while visiting Daddy's kin, and she's got a voice to soothe your head and make your heart hope.

Emmett loves Roberto Clemente, but I love Patsy Cline. Why, just tonight we listened to Patsy sing a spell on the *Grand Ole Opry Hour* on our old Philco radio like we do every Saturday night. I surely do wish we could get a TV too, but Mama says there's no call to bring a noise box into our lives when we already got a fine radio. Not only can we not afford a television set, she says, but how are we supposed to get reception in our holler? I guess we'd need an extra-large antenna. Still, I've seen televisions advertised in the Sears & Roebuck catalog, and it seems to me that if Daddy could write his hit banjo song, we might could get us one.

From my secret place in the tree, I hear Appelonia whimper from the drawer, and Mama goes to her and starts in singing about the Swannanoa Tunnel in Asheville caving in and the cold wind. It's an awful sad song for such a little one, but the new baby eats up Mama's singing and drifts on back to sleep.

Mama and Daddy say that, for the time being, Appelonia needs to sleep in the drawer and soon Mathew the Mennonite will bring us more bunk beds and an extra crib that Daddy hired him to make. The Mennonites are real nice folks who drive black trucks and, sometimes, black cars. I know this for a fact cause Daddy sold our red Opel Kadette to Mathew's brother Martin for a dollar. Next time we saw Martin, he waved to us from the Opel Kadette that he'd painted black himself. Daddy thought this was funny to see his red car now painted black and said that one day he might write a song about it. I get my songwriting from Daddy, who plans on selling a banjo hit any day now, so we can eat regular. Daddy taught me to pick on the guitar and says I can write a song about most anything on this big earth.

The soft breathing of my sisters and brothers wafts out of the window, and I'm glad to be out in the red maple where I can hear the rush of the creek from way down in the holler. I wrap my arms and legs around a branch that brushes up against the side of the house and listen to the serenade of crickets, cicadas, and tree frogs. I try not to think about being hungry, yet I have discovered that when a person is powerful hungry, blacks seem blacker, blues bluer, and yellow seems to shimmer with dancing fairies in cool moonlight. I love breathing in the colors that take my mind off the growling in my belly.

When I hear the crackling sound of fresh coal from the old potbellied stove on the porch, I peek down through the leaves to where Daddy is stoking the fire with an iron poker. The landlord left us two stoves to use, but Daddy prefers the stove on the porch, because he says warm summer nights and roasted peanuts are key ingredients for new songs. I watch him as he roasts his snack of peanuts in a cast-iron skillet on top of the potbellied stove. He eats a few while he plucks on the banjo. Daddy says hot roasted peanuts with a little salt give him song ideas. He also eats roasted peanuts when he's nervous, and he has that job interview in the morning for a part-time banjo player. It's not exactly an interview. It's more of a tryout to get his foot in the door on the *Cas Walker Farm and Home Hour* on the radio. I know for a fact that Daddy wants that job something fierce even if it means strumming the banjo to commercials about lettuce and cereal. He figures Cas Walker today, Grand Ole Opry tomorrow. Mama wants him to get it too, as maybe Mr. Walker will toss in some free groceries to boot. Lord, they say Mr. Walker has around twenty-seven grocery stores. I went to one of Cas Walker's stores once, and a sign next to a bunch of cans of lard said, "Our customers are like squirrels. They save for the winter!" Once in a while, Mr. Walker tosses live chickens off the roof into the parking lot, and the customers who catch them get to keep them.

"Daddy," I whisper down to him from the tree. "You scared about your tryout for Mr. Walker's show in the morning?"

Daddy clutches at his heart like I scared him something fierce, but then he smiles up at me on the red maple branch. "Lord-a-God. Who is that hoot owl squawking at me at midnight?"

"Can't sleep. I've tried."

"Is that a fact now? What's running through your addled brain, my sweet magnolia blossom baby?" Daddy gets closer to the tree. "Here, give me your hand."

I reach down and he scoops a warm bunch of peanuts up into my palm.

"Help you sleep . . . listen here, can you keep a secret, Livy Two? I sent off a crop of brand-new songs to the music folks in Nashville who know how to recognize hits when they hear them. It might take a while, but one is bound to sell. You can bet on that."

"I bet more than one song, Daddy," I whisper as I squeeze the peanuts in my hand. I eat the peanuts real slow, making each one last. Then I crawl into my bed through the window and yank the quilt with me. It rips up the side—not bad, but enough.

"Heard that," hisses Becksie.

"Hush up," I whisper back, but I hope Mama hasn't heard too. Maybe I can get Becksie to help me sew it up come morning if I do something sweet for her. I can hook a worm on a fishing pole or tie a knot, but I'm all butterfingers at sewing.

I curl up next to my sister Louise and smell the gypsum and clay on her hands from the homemade paint she mixes from wild berries to paint her pictures. I slip my arm out of the blankets to rest my fingertips on the stack of books from the lending library truck in Maggie Valley. Emily Dickinson poems, *Leaves of Grass* by Walt Whitman, poems by e.e. cummings, and a book about a kid called Huckleberry Finn, and another, *Go Tell It on the Mountain,* by James Baldwin. I figured I should read that one since I live on a mountain, but another favorite of mine is a photography book of exotic places. That's the title too—*Exotic Places.* It's a silly thing, I suppose, to say that a book can soothe a body, but it's the truth. I guess my most favorite is a book of Grimm's Fairy Tales because I just eat up scary stories of wicked witches, sleeping princesses, evil stepmothers, spinning needles, golden axes, brambles, and dwarves. I even make up my own stories for the little ones about fairies who live in our holler. The twins believe they have seen the fairies dancing above the sunflowers near the creek, even though Becksie and Jitters like to say it's not true —not a whiff of it—but who cares what they say? Sometimes I take the little ones on fairy hunts.

But before I go to sleep at night, I need my books stacked up beside me where I can drift off reading the titles. I love the lending library lady, Miss Attickson, who always saves books for me and old magazines. I like to read the newspapers at the lending library truck too, especially the headlines. Last one I read was a few weeks old, and it said that Martin Luther King and some other men were sentenced to spend four days in jail in Albany, Georgia, or pay $178 each for demonstrating for civil rights. Mr. King and his friends chose jail and he wrote a letter from his jail cell, which stirred folks up even more. Daddy says Martin Luther King is a fine man who fights for civil rights. I don't know what those are, but Mama says that they're strictly for folks with enough food to eat and time to mess with politics. I fall asleep with the smoky, sweet taste of peanuts in my mouth. Part of a song comes to me in my dreams:

On a yellow crackling fire
Daddy sprinkles salt on his peanuts
that sizzle and pop in the pan.
Then he shares some with Mama
on the old porch at midnight.

Daddy's roasted peanuts are so fine.
Daddy's roasted peanuts are divine.
Smells of wood smoke and midnight,
tastes of summer and mountain climes.
Daddy's roasted peanuts are so fine. . . .

CHAPTER TWO

Mama's Biscuits

Daddy leaves early for his Cas Walker audition in the car that he borrowed from Grandma Horace. A while back, he hitched a ride to Grandma Horace's house over in Enka after our Rambler gasped its last breath of life. He was only going to keep it a short while, but the days have turned into weeks, and Grandma Horace, Mama's mama, just sent us an itching mad letter dotted with lots of exclamation points and a few Bible quotes, swearing she's gonna head this way to reclaim her Chevy. Daddy's hanging on to it in the meantime, crisscrossing the Smokies at high speeds to find himself a job over in Knoxville. I ain't seen Grandma Horace since I was seven. I don't even recollect what she looks like anymore. She only let Daddy borrow her car on the condition that she's allowed to visit us again. She and Mama had a falling out when Grandma Horace called Daddy a "no-account musician" one too many times, and Mama told her that she might ought to mind her own business, and that's when Grandma Horace quit visiting or having us to visit her. But now Grandma Horace says she's afraid her grandchildren are growing up wild, and she aims to be a part of our lives again. Grandma Horace had a wild brother, Uncle Buddy, who left home some forty-odd years ago without a word, and she don't want a repeat with our family. Sometimes, I think about Uncle Buddy and wonder if he was wild, or if he maybe had an ache in his bones to see exotic lands too? I'll have to ask him if I ever meet him.

As Daddy pulls out of the holler, we chase after the car calling, "Good luck!" Becksie yells, "Bring us back something good!" and Jitters echoes, "Yeah, something good!" I pray that he comes home "gainfully employed" as Mama says. Mama calls from the front porch, "And Tom, be sure to tell 'em you got kids who need to eat! Show 'em you're the best banjo picker in Tennessee and North Carolina."

"Yes ma'am." Daddy toots the horn.

"Appeal to their conscience if they got one, Tom!"

"Darling, I've got to get on the road." Daddy blows the horn and waves.

But Mama isn't finished. "And be sure to go easy on my mama's car, or we won't never hear the end of it." Daddy guns it out of the holler down the winding road. Mama sighs and shakes her head. Daddy couldn't go easy on a car if he tried. She picks up red yarn and starts in knitting. Grandma Horace always sends Mama skeins of yarn from the Woolworth's in Enka-Stinka. They may not speak, but Grandma Horace knows Mama knits, so she always sends up heaps of yarn every color under the sun. She sends other things too. The biggest thing Grandma Horace sent was a refrigerator with a little freezer a few months back. She had it sent up the mountain to the Greyhound Bus pickup, and Mathew the Mennonite carried it over to us in his truck even though the Mennonites don't use refrigerators.

"Who's that sweater for?" I ask.

"I ain't decided yet," Mama says, needles click-clacking away. "Now don't—"

"Say Mama?" I ask, still thinking of my wild great-uncle. "What do you suppose ever happened to Uncle Buddy, Grandma Horace's brother? You think he had the wanderlust blood in him? I read somewhere that folks who like to hit the road and see the world got bit early in life by the wanderlust bug."

"I done told you what I know, Livy Two. Folks say he caught the railroad out west. Either way, he don't call and he don't write. Now get dressed. Blackberries won't pick their selves."

After a blazing morning of picking blackberries in this hot sun and keeping a lookout for hidden hornets' nests, I try to read the book *Exotic Places* to the twins Caroline and Cyrus, but they won't sit still a minute. All they care about is collecting roly-poly bugs. I don't know why I feel the need to shove some learning into their little kid brains. I try to point out the pictures to Gentle too, but her eyes won't focus on the zebras of Africa or the sands of Tibet either. When I put the book in her hands, she only grabs at the pages with her fingers.

A knot tightens in my innards when I think about my little sister's eyes the color of lilacs. She is my secret worry, because she doesn't blink when the sun shines on her face. I feel this icy wind whistling through my chest if I think about it too long. I keep hoping to see Gentle squint her baby eyes when the sun dazzles down into the holler.

I tickle her feet now, and she hugs my neck. Gentle fills my heart with a sweetness I do not understand. Mama and Daddy settled on the name Gentle on account of how easy and happy she came into the world. Daddy says she was out in two pushes and curled up on

Mama like a little tree frog. She had a mess of dark curls when she was born that have since turned yellow-gold. Since I've read my share of fairy tales, I know about maidens with fine-spun hair. Sometimes, I think that if Livy One had growed up to be a kid, she woulda looked like Gentle.

Mama doesn't seem worried about Gentle, but she's got plenty of other children to tangle with, and she don't mind telling you so. We all know Gentle's eyes don't work right, but nobody talks about it. It's like if we talk about it, it will somehow make it true.

I look over at Louise painting pictures of wild mountain flowers—sunflowers, a black-eyed Susan, Queen Anne's lace. Louise is just younger than me, but we're so close in age, we're a little like twins too. We were even born in the same year. I'm January, and she's October. For two months of the year, we're exactly the same age. Sometimes, I want to freeze my sisters and brothers in my mind. Then I wonder, does Gentle see our faces? Does she see the colors in Louise's paintings?

Emmett strolls into the holler with a mess of catfish on his fishing line and dumps them into a bucket on the front porch. Next he sits on the porch and starts in whittling on a stick with his pocketknife. No telling what it will be, as Emmett can whittle till the cows come home and that's the truth. He sculpts wooden dolls for the little ones and carves birds for Mama to put on the windowsill.

As Becksie and Jitters lug a basket of wet clothes across the front porch to hang on the line, I call to the twins, "Don't you want to hear more stories from this here book?"

Cyrus yells, "Nope! No more China or queen of England stories."

"Yeah!" says Caroline. "We're sick of them!"

I say, "Well then, just go on and be ignorant then!"

"Heck, I don't even know what ignorant means!" Cyrus shouts, but Emmett says, "Livy Two, just let them play."

"Fine, play!" I yell. "Who cares about China or Africa or Australia? They're just far-off, exotic places you'uns will probably never see anyway, but I will, I swear, I will!"

"Send us a postcard when you get there," Emmett says with a grin.

"Heck, you ain't going nowhere, Livy Two," says Becksie, a clothespin clamped in her teeth like a cigar. "You'll find a boy and get married. We all will, just like Mama and Daddy did."

"Yeah, just like them!" Jitters drapes a sheet over her head like a veil and sings, "Here comes the bride," but she trips and tumbles into the dirt, clean sheet and all.

"Ha!" I say, "I'm going to visit every last one of those exotic places, see if I don't, and I ain't dragging no husband along with me and you can bet on that!" But for the moment, I give up trying to educate anyone in this family and set *Exotic Places* on the smokehouse window. Maybe I ought to switch back to fairy tales for a while.

After a pitiful lunch of turnip greens and a few slivers of fatback, the little kids are supposed to take naps, but it's too hot to sleep, so they slip outside to join me under the shade of the red maple, while Mama drowses with Appelonia on the porch swing. Sometimes, it seems like these summer days might could last forever. I tie Gentle on my back in a sling piggyback style, to pass the time. I say to the twins, "Watch this June bug trick." I teach them how to tie a June bug to a string and let it fly around. They shriek with laughter at the buzzing June bug, but Gentle doesn't even notice.

"I'm still hungry as a wolf." Emmett plays his harmonica, and the notes actually sound like hunger, all jagged and lonesome. "As usual."

Caroline, eyes as big as saucers, says, "Don't talk about wolves," but Cyrus yells, "I'll fight the wolves. I'll fight them all!" If Cyrus and Caroline looked any more alike, they'd be the same person, even if they are boy and girl. They wear matching overalls too. All of us wear overalls day in and day out, except Becksie and Jitters. Nothing but old gingham dresses sent up from Grandma Horace's church bazaar sales will do for them two queen bees. You couldn't pay me a dollar to wear an Enka-Stinka girly dress.

"So you think you'll fight all the wolves?" Emmett swings around Cyrus, who squeals with laughter. "Why, you ain't nothing but a roly-poly bug yourself." Emmett's fourteen, the oldest of us kids, hemmed in by so many sisters. I think Emmett plays rough with Cyrus to get him to grow up faster, but Cyrus loves every minute of it.

"Higher, Emmett, higher! I'm huge like a giant!" Cyrus tries to stick his chest out.

Emmett says, "Sure you are, buddy. Heck, I'm so hungry, I could eat fifty wolves." He sets Cyrus down and plays his harmonica, the sweet sound weaves its way under my skin.

Becksie takes the dried sheets off the line and snaps, "Don't be talking about food. We won't feel so hungry."

Emmett asks, "Lord, Lady Becksie, what's it like to have all the answers?"

"I can't help it if I have the most brains in this family," Becksie replies.

"Yeah, she cain't help it being smartest!" Jitters stomps her foot. Jitters would like to be as old as Becksie instead of younger than Louise. They both wear their brown braids wound so tight it seems like their temples might pop.

Before Emmett can toss them both into the creek, which is about what they deserve, I yell, "Y'all quit. Lookee here. I, at least, got one answer." I pull out an extra pail of blackberries from the crawl space under the house. "Shhh! Don't let Mama see." They all dive toward the pail anyway. "I told her we only picked two pails, not three."

They're too busy eating to answer. I don't eat any, because I've already stuffed myself with so many blackberries I got a bellyache. I feel ashamed that I ate more than my share, but I did pick extra for everyone. At least that's what I tell myself to ease the guilty pricks. I wish I weren't so lowdown greedy. It's my biggest, ugliest fault. Here I look like Robin Hood bringing blackberries to the hungry, but that's about as far from the truth as a body could get. I washed my face earlier to clean away the evidence.

But the kids are too hungry to notice that I don't eat. Even Lady Becksie rips into the juicy berries like a black bear cub, and so I'm hoping she'll agree to sew my quilt for me. After the pail is empty, I make everyone head toward the creek to scrub their faces and purple-stained fingers, or else Mama will know the truth at supper. We'll have more salted fatback from the smokehouse in the black-eyed peas along with Emmett's catfish. Fatback can be a little rubbery, but it flavors up the peas real good.

By late afternoon, Daddy still isn't home, but Mama says she ain't surprised. She says he might not even be back until tomorrow. "I bet Daddy gets that job on Cas Walker's radio show," I say, wishing our father would magically appear, his pockets spilling over with gold coins like Ali Baba in *Arabian Nights*, one of the best stories ever written. "I bet that's what is taking him so long. They want to hear all his banjo songs and make him rich as heaven."

Emmett's face hardens into flinty meanness, and I reckon it's because he's been hearing about the banjo hit the longest. He is sick to death of waiting for it to happen. I don't mention how Daddy sent another crop of songs off to the Nashville music folks.

Louise says, "I sure wish he'd sell it already."

Becksie says, "Then we could eat anything anytime."

"Quit flapping your jaws about it!" Emmett snaps. "Makes me sick hearing that hit banjo song talk. I want food. I want to get fat on food. I'm sick of being hungry."

I interrupt, "Hey, know what food I'd like to try? Baked Alaska. It's a dessert with swirls of ice cream and layers of cake that you light on fire to melt the meringue."

"You made that up," Becksie says. "That's a bald-faced lie."

"Yeah," says Jitters, "you can't bake an Alaskan!"

"Baked Alaska!" I yell. "Don't you'uns know nothing at all?"

Becksie says, "Well, if we got rich, I'd give all the money to the poor."

Jitters says, "Me too."

Emmett chomps on a piece of sour grass and says, "Good God Almighty, pin a medal on you two Christian queens. For your information, we are the poor."

After a supper of catfish and black-eyed peas, I walk Gentle outside to where Louise is painting a school of dancing fish inside rainbows. One of her other dried paintings is a wild thunderstorm. As I lean closer, I say, "Gentle, there's a real witch in the picture with all the rain clouds. Wait? Hold up. Is it? It could be . . . It must be . . . Hey, Grandma Horace, how'd you fly on your broomstick and get into Louise's picture?"

Louise laughs and says, "There's no witch in my picture."

"I could have sworn she was right there in the red and black," I say.

"Crimson and ebony," Louise corrects me as she guides Gentle's fingers and lets her run them along the lines and shapes of the painting. Gentle puts her eyes close to the canvas. I wonder how much she can actually see. Gentle never talks about what she can or can't see. Is it a blur of color? Gray clouds? Blackness? Not blackness, please.

Gentle whispers, "Say about the witch again, Livy Two."

I lie back in the grass with Gentle, who crawls on my stomach and dances her fingers along my face. "You mean Grandma Horace? Well, maybe she's not in Louise's picture, but she's an old witch who lives over the mountain in Enka-Stinka, who flies on her broomstick over the smelly paper mill, and you can hear her cackling laugh and even the fairies duck when she comes swooping over across the skies, and—"

Louise shakes her head. "What if Grandma does come? Then what'll you do?"

"After all these years? Why I bet she wouldn't stick one proud city witch toe in this holler."

Mama comes out of the house, nursing Appelonia, and says, "Bed. Now."

"But Daddy's not home," I argue. "I got to wait up for him."

"Knoxville's a long way from Maggie Valley. Now come on, scrub faces, brush teeth. I already put the twins to bed. Becksie and Jitters are long asleep too. You'uns are next." Still nursing, Mama reaches for a pile of yarn and sits down in the rocking chair. "I got a lot of work to do."

"Wait, Mama." I hope to delay bedtime. "I wrote a song about you."

"I ain't got time to listen to no songs. I'm flat wore out."

"It's about the way you make biscuits into shapes."

Mama starts in knitting but says, "Well, you gonna talk it or sing it?"

I hand Gentle to Louise, and I pick up my guitar and sing Mama's song:

Mama's working hands shaping our biscuits . . .
sifting out the flour for the biscuits
pouring out the buttermilk too
reaching for the rolling pin and
spreading out the sweet dough . . .

Mama's working hands shaping our biscuits . . .
into fiddles and daisies and wheelbarrows and shovels
and cows and monsters and coiled snakes
and puppies and sunshine and stars . . .

Mama's loving hands shaping our biscuits . . .

Mama doesn't say anything. It gets quiet on the porch with the crickets and cicadas crying from the forest. Louise says, "Well, what'd you think, Mama?"

"I like it just fine." She knits and shifts Appelonia to nurse on the other side.

"Thank you, Mama. You think my singing voice is all right too?"

"It's real pretty, Livy Two," Mama says. "You know that."

"But do you think I sound like singers on the radio? Cause, I sure—"

"Now quit fishing for compliments," Mama says. "You'uns, get to bed. It's late."

Louise takes Gentle inside, and Emmett follows, but I linger at the door. I go back to Mama and put my arms around her shoulders. She keeps knitting and nursing without missing a beat. "Now what?"

"Mama, how much you reckon Gentle can see?" My mind goes to the way Gentle stood in front of Louise's painting and didn't seem to see anything.

"Hush Livy Two! You're not to worry about that. That's grown-up worries."

Mama goes inside the house to put Appelonia to bed in the shirt drawer. I try not to think about Gentle's eyes, but instead about the way Mama's cheeks turned pink as I was singing her song. And it's all true. Mama does make the best buttermilk biscuits. Why, when Daddy gets a paycheck, Mama hits the kitchen at dawn and pretty soon the whole house smells of buttery brown biscuits and black strap molasses and hot black coffee laced with honey. I wish our house could smell like that all the time. I feel safe when biscuits are baking in the oven, but they don't come cheap. Nothing does in this world, according to Mama. I wonder how long it will take for those Nashville music folks to buy my daddy's songs. I sure wish he would come home soon. As I drift off to sleep, another song comes into my head, but it's just names. Still, I hear the music in my brothers' and sisters' names as they crowd into my dreams like a swarm of butterflies.

Earnest Emmett—Bossy Becksie—Jumping Jitters—
Light of Livy One in the sky—
Lovely Louise—Clever Caroline—Scrappy Cyrus—
Gem of Gentle—

and sweet baby Appelonia.
But who am I?
Earnest Emmett—Bossy Becksie—Jumping Jitters—
Light of Livy One in the sky—
Lovely Louise—Clever Caroline—Scrappy Cyrus—
Gem of Gentle—
and sweet baby Appelonia.
But who am I? Who am I? Who am I?

CHAPTER THREE

Mathew the Mennonite

The next morning, there is still no sign of Daddy. I try to keep my mind busy, but I see Mama's eyes watching the road, too, and I get anxious along with her. Louise paints a flock of peahens on the underside of the wheelbarrow, while Becksie and Jitters water the garden. Emmett takes the car radio out of our broken Rambler and tries to coax some life back into it. For a second, a Cas Walker jingle for coal comes on the radio with an old guy announcing, "A warm rump for every lump." But the reception dies, and Emmett mutters some words we're not ever supposed to say.

As I show Gentle, Cyrus, and Caroline how to make mudpie faces near the creek, Mathew the Mennonite grinds his black truck up the hill. The Mennonite men wear straw hats and have beards, and the women wear real pretty bonnets with sky blue dresses. Mathew the Mennonite does not charge but twenty-five cents an hour for carpentry, and Daddy swears that Mathew the Mennonite is about the finest carpenter this side of the Smokies. The Mennonites get along fine with the Cherokee Indians who run the pony rides in Maggie Valley. I mean, I suppose they get along, but it's hard to know because they don't much talk to each other. There are folk in this valley who do not talk to one another. It's not a hatred so far as I can tell, but more of a toleration, Daddy says, cause folks got to live together and get along. Most folks will say "Howdy" to us on the road, but since we're not natives of Maggie Valley, there are others won't even nod or look us in the eye. We are a curiosity, since we've only lived here a year or so, and Daddy says you can't be considered a native until you've lived here near a hundred years.

As Mathew the Mennonite climbs out of his truck, Louise takes one look at him and hightails it off into the woods. That girl is terrible shy around folks who ain't blood, but not me. It's like I'm hungry to talk to people, strangers or not. I call, "Hey, Mr. Mathew, you want to see Mama?" But before I can move toward the house, Becksie and Jitters run inside yelling, "Mama! Mathew the Mennonite is here. He done brung the beds."

As Mathew the Mennonite totes the crib off the truck onto his back, I bring the little ones up from the creek and settle them onto the porch, wet and muddy. "Wait here," I order as I catch up to him. "Say, Mr. Mathew, I been meaning to ask you how your girls are doing these days." Mr. Mathew has two daughters that I've been longing to meet, but they stick close to home.

"They're all right." He heads inside the house with the furniture.

"I reckon we're all about the same age." I shadow him into the sitting room near the old Philco radio. "Say, don't you think it's funny I never met them before? What are their names again?"

"Ruth and Sarah."

"Ruth and Sarah. Fine names. Are they shy, your girls? My sister Louise, now, she's shy too, but even if your girls are, they wouldn't have to be shy around me. You ought to bring them with you. We could have us a good time up in the field."

Mama calls from the bedroom, "Livy Two, don't talk the poor man to death."

"I ain't talking him to death, am I, Mr. Mathew?

We're just having a conversation. Mr. Mathew, do you rent or own your land?"

"Well . . . we own it." Mathew the Mennonite begins to sand the legs of the bed.

"That's a good thing. Boy, not us. I guess we been renters forever. Why, Daddy moved us to Maggie Valley so the landlord in Tuxedo wouldn't find us. Or was it East Flat Rock? One of them towns anyway. See that yellow patchwork quilt on the wall?" I point. "That's from East Flat Rock."

"Hush, Livy Two," Mama calls from the kitchen. "Don't be bothering Mr. Mathew. Go outside and clean up the babies now. They're waiting on you."

I nod, but I don't want to fool with those messy old kids. I want to keep talking to Mathew the Mennonite. "Do you have enough food to eat in your family, Mr. Mathew?"

"I reckon we do."

"Then you're a lucky man, sir, cause a body can sure get tired of eating turnips all the livelong day."

"Livelong ain't a word," Becksie pipes up from the window.

"Yeah, it ain't a word, so there!" echoes the echo, Jitters.

I ignore the snooping spies as I explain the word to Mathew the Mennonite. "Livelong is so a word, ain't it, Mr. Mathew? This poet, Emily Dickinson, uses 'livelong' in her poem called 'I'm Nobody.' It goes, 'I'm nobody! Who are you? Are you nobody too?' Of course, she's not the only poet I like. I like another poet by the name of e.e. cummings. You ever heard of him?"

"I don't reckon so." Mr. Mathew keeps right on sanding the legs.

"You should read him then. Read him to your girls. He wrote a poem about daffodils, lilacs, and roses. He don't capitalize nothing when he writes his poems down."

"Is that a fact?"

"Yes, it is . . . and he also wrote a poem that goes like this: 'maggie and milly and molly and may went down to the beach (to play one day).' Say, do you like fairy tales?"

"Olivia Hyatt Weems!" Mama appears behind me and grabs me by the straps of my overalls and says, "I told you to leave that poor man in peace. Go give the children some cornbread and buttermilk, but crumble the cornbread into the buttermilk, don't cut slices. There's not enough to go around, hear me?"

Mathew the Mennonite says, "Nice talking with you, Olivia."

I say, "Likewise. You be sure to tell your daughters

I said hey and that I look forward to meeting them one day. Oh, I almost forgot. I also like the poet Robert Frost. He wrote one called 'Ghost House' which gives me the shivers. You ever—"

Mama chases me out of the room and says, "Not another word, miss!"

I walk outside to wash up the twins and Gentle on the porch, but I think of the way Mathew the Mennonite said my name. *Olivia*. After I scrub the kids up with a soapy rag and dry them clean as a whistle, I break up bits of cornbread into glasses and pour buttermilk into each glass and pass out spoons to the kids.

I try to not eat more than my share, but then I pretend to drop something and shove a big piece of cornbread into my mouth under the table. Nobody catches me, but I feel guilty as I swallow fast. I shouldn't be so awful greedy, I know it. The cornbread crumbs tickle my throat, and I want to cough, but I don't dare. I go to the spring and gulp pure mountain water to wash it down before Mama catches me.

I look down at the empty road. Still no car, nothing. Maybe Daddy stopped off to play in a honky-tonk or maybe he's picked up extra jars of baby food or encyclopedias to sell on the way back from the tryout. One time, at a honky-tonk, some men threw beer bottles at him and the other musicians, but luckily nobody got

hurt bad. But lately he's also been working as a traveling salesman out of the trunk of Grandma Horace's car.
Once I went with him on his rounds, and the baby food
went a sight quicker than the encyclopedias, though
Daddy always reminded folks, "You'uns ought to feed
your children's brains as well as their stomachs."

But some folks didn't appreciate being told this, and
more than one told Daddy to mind his own business,
only they said it in meaner ways like, "Why the hell
don't you mind your own business?" Mama says we're
not supposed to say the word "hell." On the day we sold
the baby food and encyclopedias, we took a break to
drink sweet tea at Maggie's Diner and wrote songs
together. We only ordered sweet tea because that way
we could get free refills. Daddy sketched our waitress,
who had eyes traveling in different directions, but he
made her look pretty anyway.

Suddenly, I hear the sound of the sputtering muffler, and by some miracle, it is Daddy—I pray he got the
Cas Walker job. Please, oh please! He pulls into our
holler with Grandma's muffler spitting and coughing
up a storm of black smoke and parks next to Mathew
the Mennonite's truck. Then the funniest sight happens.

Daddy opens the passenger door and whistles, and
the silliest dog scrambles out of the car, wagging his

tail and barking to beat the band. He's a funny little sausage dog with red tawny fur. Daddy grins and says, "Howdy you'uns. This here young feller is Uncle Hazard. Say how-do, young hot dog. A man from Hazard, Kentucky, give him to me at a gas pump in Knoxville."

We all run toward the dog, who leaps up to greet us. He jumps on Becksie, leaving paw prints on her Enka-Stinka dress, and she screams like an old lady, which makes Jitters holler too. Then Emmett asks what we all want to know. "Did the Cas Walker radio folks give you the job, Daddy?"

Daddy peers at the ground for a second, blinking like he's got something caught in his eye. "Much to my dismay, son, they gave it to someone else. Naturally, the man can't pick worth a lick, but . . . what can I do? They plan to contact me again."

I try not to cry as I bury my face in the new dog's neck. Then Daddy says, "But you'uns don't need to fret. That just means another banjo job is in the works. And you can trust your old daddy, I got plenty of other fish frying up right now. Shoot, I got me all sorts of songs and melodies in my head."

Mama stands on the front porch, nostrils flaring like the ponies' at the pony rides in Maggie Valley, but she can't yell at Daddy in front of Mathew the

Mennonite. However, Mr. Mathew seems to size up the situation real quick and announces, "Beds are ready. You can pay me later. Nice seeing you, Mr. Weems." He climbs into his truck.

As soon as Mathew the Mennonite cranks the engine and eases out of the holler, our soft-spoken Mama up and roars at Daddy like a grizzly, "Tom, I don't know what you're thinking bringing a dog into this holler!" She grabs up an empty sack of cornmeal from the porch and waves it like a flag. "We don't hardly have enough food to feed our children as it is, so I'm telling you this right now—no dogs. No dogs!" Her face is raw, with streaks of burgundy in her cheeks. She turns back to us, "You'uns children are not to get attached to this animal. You hear me? It ain't staying. I ain't feeding it."

I bite my lip and blink back the tears. Uncle Hazard is far too busy poking and sniffing to notice he ain't exactly welcome. Then he spies Louise coming out of the woods and gallops up to her to introduce himself. She can come out of hiding now that Mathew the Mennonite is gone. "Hey dog, hey dog." She smiles and pats the pup, but then Daddy starts yelling back at Mama. "I'll tell you what I was thinking, Jessie." Daddy slams the car door. "I was thinking that these kids need a dog, and this one here showed up out of the blue.

Dogs and children belong together. That is my candid belief."

"Where is your candid belief regarding gainful employment?" Mama snaps, her eyes red. "It ain't fitten to have a dog when we got mouths we can't barely feed."

"He's little. He ain't gonna eat much. All I'm saying is that—"

"I know what you're saying, Tom, and until we don't have to discuss the fact that we got a baby sleeping in a shirt drawer and children with empty stomachs more often than not, we'll have no more foolish dog talk."

As she stomps back into the house, Daddy's jaw starts working. He grabs up a chair like he's going to smash it against the pitiful washing machine on the porch, but then he sets it down careful and gets out his banjo. He chomps on peanuts from his pocket in order to keep his temper. This fight ain't over, not by a lick. I know Mama loves Daddy, but she sees that dog as nothing but trouble.

The funny sausage dog dashes around the holler in crazed exploration, sobs of excitement in his throat. He tries to catch a grasshopper and then stops short to bay at a fat greenish toad. He sees a cardinal and springs after it down the holler. His little legs move fast for a body so close to the ground. I look at Emmett who grins as he watches that dog with the short legs run. I run to chase down the dog who might belong to us for at least a few hours. Then Gentle sways as I skip past her, so I stop and ask, "What are you doing, Gentle?" She makes sounds like "Whooooshhh, swwwiisssssh." I stop and listen, and then I hear it . . . a soft breeze in the treetops. Gentle is playing like she's the wind.

CHAPTER FOUR

Grandma's Glass Eyes

The next day, Daddy takes off before daylight. He doesn't even wait for coffee. He's just gone again, and he don't take Uncle Hazard with him, which means he is throwing down the gauntlet like those medieval knights used to do in the old days. Since the Cas Walker job didn't happen, he's got a heap of baby food jars and encyclopedias to sell 'fore Mama starts talking to him again. We eat grits for breakfast and pretend we might get to keep Uncle Hazard, even though Mama says, "Dog? What dog?" as she knits a blue sweater with bits of green.

I don't dare to laugh, even though I see Uncle Hazard's black nose snuffling under the back door for crumbs.

After breakfast, me and Emmett and Louise hitch a plan to hide Uncle Hazard and hope for the best. We bring Gentle along to help us build a little dog-house of sticks down in the sally grass near the creek, about a half mile from the house. We decorate the doghouse with pinecones and redbud leaves. Gentle puts bigger pinecones in one pile and smaller ones in another pile. We call the house Uncle Hazard's pine-cone palace. Louise paints a sign and hangs it above his front door. I throw in a burlap sack to keep him warm at night. The pinecone palace is really more of a lean-to than an actual house, but Uncle Hazard seems right pleased with it.

The sun burns down hot on our backs as the creek water rushes by with honeyed dapples of sunlight. When we finish the palace, we take off our overalls and climb into the water to cool off. I carry Gentle into the water too, and she loves the icy water splashing on her feet and legs. But Uncle Hazard stays on the bank where it's dry, barking and pacing the banks like some officer of the law. It's clear that Uncle Hazard is one dog who hates water. When all the coaxing and begging in the world don't get him into the water, Emmett scoops the pup up for a swim, but as soon as the water hits Uncle Hazard, he shivers and whines like it's pure acid torture. Louise says, "Aw, let him go, Emmett. He hates it. Look at him." Uncle Hazard yelps and wriggles out of Emmett's arms like a slippery whistle pig. He swims ashore, shakes himself off, and rolls in the dirt clean away from the water and snuggles into his pine-cone palace, a lone wet tail sticking out.

Mama does not know about Uncle Hazard's creek-side pinecone palace, and we aim to keep it that way. Can't let Becksie or Jitters catch wind or the word will spread all over the place, and best not to let the twins know neither.

Later that day, Daddy comes home armed with flour, eggs, butter, sugar, and a sack of coconut shavings. He also hands Mama a sack of knitting yarn for more sweaters and such. Mama sits on the porch shucking corn, quiet, so Daddy says, "How about this, Jessie?"

Mama keeps right on shucking. Becksie and Jitters shuck right along with her in perfect rhythm like angels. Carolyn and Cyrus push Gentle on the tire swing. Emmett's off fishing with Louise. I sit up hidden in the leaves of the red maple and try to keep reading my book about Huckleberry Finn sailing down the Mississippi River on a raft.

I already read the biography of Mark Twain once, and I learned that Mark Twain's wife had the same name as me—Livy. But to tell you the truth, I feel more like Mark Twain than I do his wife Livy because Mr.

Twain wasn't much for sitting around. But it's hard to concentrate on the story while a-waiting for the front porch fireworks display between Mama and Daddy.

"Looks good, don't it?" Daddy tries again, but Mama still don't answer.

Becksie says, "Where'd you get this food, Daddy?"

"Yeah, where?" Jitters wants to know.

"This, my lovely daughters, was donated," Daddy says, a smile dancing at his lips.

"Donated?" Mama's eyebrows raise up into triangle tips.

I slide down out of the maple to get a closer look at the food. "It ain't a handout either," Daddy says, reading Mama's mind. "Put on your baking hat, gal, and get ready to bake some layer cakes for Settlers Days. I was minding my own business selling that baby food up and down the streets of Maggie Valley, see, and some old boys come up and asked me to be a kind of Masters of Talent at Settlers Days. This is like a job. I get to choose the mountain talent. Heck, I'll probably pick a little myself for the folks. You never know when opportunity may knock. Right? Anyhow, I guess they like the way I sing about baby food and try to raffle off jars in the town. And so, look at all this extra food. This is a month's worth of supplies. Maybe more, knowing how you can make things stretch, Jessie."

"Ha."

"It's like bonus food as a reward or a thank-you—for making the cakes. We got beans, honey, flour, cornmeal, coffee, lard, preserves."

"I can see what we got, Tom," Mama says, unimpressed.

"Well, it's not bad in exchange for just a few cakes. I told the folks that my wife was one of the best cake-makers ever to grace Maggie Valley. That her eight-layer coconut cake and applesauce cake were rare glimpses into heaven itself. Get it started though. Cake raffle is in a few days."

"Does the job pay in anything besides flour and sugar and lard?" Mama asks.

"Does it pay? Heck, Jessie, I'm going to be making all kinds of contacts. Don't you see, this is a start toward gainful employment? We're still new to these parts. Folks meet you. See what you're about. Next thing you know—"

"I'd prefer a paycheck in hand." Mama finishes shucking the corn and pours soap into the dancing washing machine and whacks it with the broom.

"Lord have mercy, don't I know it." Daddy winks at us.

After we sing "Amen" to bless our supper, Daddy says,

"This is some delicious victuals. Black-eyed peas bring you luck, children."

Louise says, "I guess we're storing up a lot of luck."

"Manners, Miss," Mama warns.

"If Grandma Horace ever comes to claim her car, you reckon she'll bring her collection of glass eyes?" I aim to steer the talk in another direction.

"Yeah," Louise says. "I'd like to paint a picture of her and her glass eyes."

Becksie wails, "I'm trying to eat. Quit talking about eyeballs."

"Me too! No eyeball talk!" Jitters's fork clatters to the floor.

"Yuck, eyeballs!" Caroline moans, but Cyrus says, "What color eyeballs?"

Then I hear it. From far down in the holler, I hear the low, soft howl of Uncle Hazard, but I pretend it's nothing. "Baaaaaaaawhhhhooooooo!"

Mama hums "In the Pines" a little louder than usual, and I can tell she's pretending not to hear a peep of howling. That would mean admitting that Uncle Hazard is still around, and she wants our fine dog gone yesterday and that's a fact.

"He sounds lonesome," Louise says. "He can make the 'B' sound with his howl."

"That's talent for you." Emmett soaks up the last

of his black-eyed peas with a hunk of cornbread. "Well, I'm still starving. As usual. I think this lack of food has stunted my growth. I ought to be six feet tall by now instead of five foot four inches."

"Don't start." Mama eats one more bite of black-eyed peas and puts the rest on Emmett's plate. "Vegetables will be ready to pick in another month or so. And Tom, I got one thing to say. That animal you carried all the way from Knoxville is gone come morning. I mean it. It's me or the dog."

"Jessie, please," Daddy says, but Mama keeps right on eating her cornbread, one calm bite after another. Appelonia nurses while Mama eats. The baby sure can eat, and Mama never does one thing when she can do two, three, four things at once.

Uncle Hazard continues to bay from his pinecone palace.

"He sounds sad. I bet he misses Kentucky," Caroline whimpers, tears in her eyes.

"He can have my food," Cyrus offers. "I ain't hungry."

Mama gives Daddy a hard look, and his mouth twitches this way and that as he tries to think of an idea. Finally, he says, "All right. I'm sorry, children, but your Mama is right. I'll have to find a temporary new home for Uncle Hazard."

Then we all start in howling and crying, but Mama keeps right on eating.

"Mama," Emmett says, "I could teach Hazard to catch fish. We'd have enough food." He pounds his fork on the table to get her attention. We all yell in agreement.

Daddy shouts over the din, "You'uns hush. Your Mama is right. I need to sell a big banjo hit before we get a dog."

"Even a little one, Tom," Mama says. "I'd take that."

Daddy says, "Don't think small now, Mrs. Jessie Weems."

Emmett shouts, "Daddy, how many times do we got to hear about this banjo hit? Either sell it or quit talking about it. It's more than a body can stand." He bolts from the table before Daddy can say a word. I hear my brother whistle for Uncle Hazard, and I know he's racing down toward the pinecone palace to be alone with our dog. Daddy pushes the food around on his plate, but he doesn't go after Emmett.

Sick of all this money talk, I start to clear the table without being asked. Supper never lasts long at our house. No meal does. I scrub the dishes and cast my mind back to Grandma Horace's glass eyes. I can still recollect seeing them when I was a kid. She keeps a collection in the drawer by her bed and claims she lost her real eye from a tumor, because it sounds more ladylike, but everyone knows her long-lost brother, Buddy, misfired a slingshot at her as a child. I make up the first verse about Grandma's eyes.

Grandma lost her eye when she was just a girl.
Now she's got six glass eyes, and one looks like a pearl.
Grandma's got an eye like a pearl.
Grandma's got an eye like a pearl.

I ain't thought up the rest yet. Uncle Hazard bays again from the bottom of the holler, and Gentle perks up her ears and laughs. "Uncle Hazard's funny."

CHAPTER FIVE

Floating Checks

*M*ama, Becksie, and Jitters need to start on the coconut cake, since the three applesauce cakes are done. The aroma from the kitchen smells heavenly. I been out working in the garden, and I'm beat. Gentle plays near me under an old umbrella, chewing on a tomato. "How's that tomato, little gal?" I ask.

"Yum." Gentle grins and takes another bite.

I water the Kentucky Wonders, which'll be ready to pick when they're 'bout long as your arm. Next, I weed the yellow crookneck squash and the spring onions and finally the sweet white corn, which is always good, but can be a heap a trouble, cutting up your arms with those leaves. I can almost taste how good the corn will be in another month or so. I also got to pick the bugs and weeds out of the peppers and tomatoes or else they'll get all twisted up and funny-shaped. We eat turnip or mustard greens in the summer, but come winter, it's collard greens, yellow onions, and potatoes.

As I get me and Gentle a drink of cool water from the spring, I hear a wild snarling from Uncle Hazard up near his pinecone palace. But this time, it ain't no howling. This is a wallop of fearsome cries, as if Uncle Hazard is scared clean to the bone. Mama is sure to hear him, too, and know Daddy forgot him. Again.

I grab up Gentle and take her into the kitchen where I hand her off to Becksie, who starts to squawk as usual, but I fly out of the house before she can try to stop me. I meet Emmett running from the other direction, and we hit the path toward the creek and round the bend together, where we spy a sight that stops us dead in our tracks. A big old mama bear snuffles around Uncle Hazard's pinecone palace. She inches closer to Uncle Hazard, who barks all ferocious at the bear like he's some old coon dog who's treed a skunk or squirrel or something.

As I watch the bear get closer, I feel my blood turn to icicles like the ones that hang off the bluffs come winter. I've only had this hot dog a day or so, and it looks like he is going to be a snack for a mama bear even though anybody with a lick of sense knows bears don't eat dogs. They eat blackberries and blueberries and whatever else they can scrounge up on the mountain. But that mama bear has a look in her eye, and I know it is a mama bear because not ten feet from us is her cub, having a frolic in the creek. Uncle Hazard isn't having any of it, and he circles the bear, playing the tough dog, hair standing up on his back in hackles of fury.

"Get back, Uncle Hazard!" I shout, but Emmett silences me, because sure enough, that old mama bear turns an eye toward us. As she does a kind of half-shuffle in our direction, Emmett shoves me up onto the branch of the nearest dogwood tree. I scale the branches with Emmett close behind me. The ground below looks smeary and full of hot yellow light as the mama bear lumbers back toward Uncle Hazard.

Then the oddest thing happens. Uncle Hazard quits barking and rolls over on his back, playing the fool as if to say, "Don't bite. I was just playing." The mama bear leans down to lick Uncle Hazard across the top of his head. And she keeps right on licking him. Pretty soon, the cub scoots up out of the water, and he and Uncle Hazard start wrestling on the bank. Uncle Hazard won't get near the creek, as that would mean getting wet, but he and the baby cub have a fine time. I can hardly believe it, this dog passing the time of day with a mama and baby bear. If only Mama could see him now, she'd know how special he was. "Emmett," I whisper. "You think Mama might change her mind about Uncle Hazard?"

"Aw, ain't nothing gonna change Mama's mind. We just got to be real sly. You know how Mama's got that big old sack of meal just off the kitchen? Well, she's not going to notice if a cup goes missing now and then."

"The heck she isn't. She keeps a measuring stick in it."

"We'll just have to take our chances then. We can cook it up at midnight."

At that moment, the mama bear and her cub lumber off up the mountain path, and Uncle Hazard scampers up the bank to see us. As soon as the coast is clear, we climb down out of the tree, and Uncle Hazard jumps up on Emmett, licking his face.

"This dog has got to learn that his house is down here by the creek. Faster he learns that, the better." Emmett takes a deep breath, and he's got a funny look on his face. "Can you keep a secret, Livy Two?" His eyes dart back and forth as if checking for spies.

"Of course I can, Emmett Weems. What do you think?"

"No fooling, this is the biggest secret of my life." His face is pink and his hair stands up like straw.

"Emmett Weems, did I tell on you the time you

chased a groundhog and slid headfirst into the creek? Did I ever breathe a word to anyone?"

He considers this a moment. "I reckon not, but this is like a pledge, Livy Two. A pledge of true and sworn loyalty. I'm treating you like I would a real brother, but Cyrus is too little for secrets or pledges."

"I swear, Emmett, I won't tell. I ain't some girly girl."

"All right then," Emmett says, "I got my eyes fixed on the new Ghost Town in the Sky."

"That place with the chairlift over the mountain?" I feel a kind of dread come over me. What's Ghost Town in the Sky got to do with us?

"I aim to get me a job there real soon."

I don't say nothing, cause I'm afraid my chest will like to bust wide open. My brother can't leave. The sun hits his yellow hair, and his hazel eyes burn with gumption.

"Say something." Emmett anchors his thumbs on the buckles of his overalls.

I take a breath and say, "A durned old chairlift don't seem the smartest way to get up on top of a mountain. No sir, not if you ask me. What if the fool thing breaks?"

But it's like Emmett ain't even listening. "They got bank robber and gunfight shows, saloon girls . . .

just like the old Wild West. A sheriff and an under-taker. All sorts. The workers shaved off seventy feet of mountain just to create this miracle, and I aim to see it for myself. Wish I coulda helped build it."

"What do you care about them saloon girls for?"

Emmett grins and picks up a stone and skips it across the creek. "I reckon I'm interested in just about everything."

Uncle Hazard wags his tail as Emmett looks out across the valley. "Livy Two, you mean to tell me you wouldn't like to sail up over a mountain toward the sky in a fancy chairlift? Three thousand, three hundred feet in the air. I bet workers eat three meals a day there too. Maybe they even got worker housing. I aim to find out."

"Why can't you live at home and work there?"

"I'm tired of living at home. Besides, who knows when Daddy will decide to up and move us again. I want some control of my life. Working a real job for real money at Ghost Town in the Sky is the best plan for me."

"Only way I know how to get up a mountain is clinging to rocks and scrabbling up branches every step of the way. That's the real way." But, in spite of myself, I feel a thrill of excitement too. It makes me think of African safaris or going off to find polar bears in Alaska. It's an adventure. Emmett wants an adventure just like me. I thought I was the only one, and I thought I'd be going first, but he's already making plans at fourteen. I don't want him to go just yet. We don't say nothing else as we watch Uncle Hazard chase a butterfly. I whisper a prayer to Livy One to bring us more food, to keep Emmett with us. Don't let him run off the way Uncle Buddy did, never to be heard from again.

"But I already know how to fix it," Jitters argues with Louise over Louise's newest painting in progress later that afternoon. Gentle snoozes on my belly while I watch the sisters' spat brewing from my secret place under the house. I got more secret places than I can count, and boyhowdy, I use them all. Only Gentle is invited to visit. I try to ignore the argument by fixing my mind on the future. I may come from a big family, but I already know I don't want children. I want my own house all to myself in the holler, and I swear I won't fill it with nothing but banjo music and vases of mountain laurel and plenty of food. My nieces and nephews will be allowed to visit on Saturdays from one to two. I want a homemade rocking chair and a granny quilt on the bed and a rug from Persia on the floor. I wouldn't mind a fancy refrigerator or, even better, a record player like other regular folks have, and I would play me all kinds of music from Patsy Cline to Mozart. Miss Attickson, the librarian from the lending library truck, always plays Mozart. Yes indeed, I'll bring the world back to my mountain cabin and write songs about all the places I've been. I might even serve up Baked Alaska every night if I feel like it, and my guests will be smart enough to know that it's a dessert and—

"Good night! Leave me be!" Louise yells at Jitters, and I scoot over to the slats in the wood under the house to get a better view of the fight.

"But it's messy," Jitters insists, and imitates the way Becksie puts her hand on her hip. "I said it would look neater if you did it this way." Then she goes and tries to clean the raspberry paint that oozes off of the painting.

Louise waves her off. "You ain't never painted a dadgummed thing in your life."

"I still know what I know, and Mama says you need to get the wheelbarrow and go yonder to collect manure from the Mennonite cows, so we can fertilize—"

"Jitters, I am going to knock the tar out of you!" Louise shouts, and Jitters skedaddles into the house. Louise snatches up her work and tears off up the mountain trail where she can't be bothered, muttering about

Mennonite cows. Poor Louise. I'll let her come visit me in my mountain cabin so she can paint in peace.

Then I hear a plate crash in the house, and Mama starts yelling. "My cake! That dog climbed right up on the table. That was a good plate! One of the few I have left!" The first thing I see is Uncle Hazard running out of the house with half an applesauce cake in his mouth. Mama chases after him with the broom, yelling, but Uncle Hazard is long gone with part of the cake. I stay hidden under the house with Gentle. What can I do? Rescue the cake? Uncle Hazard? How? How did he even get into the house? Then I peek down the path, and I see the dog running toward Emmett. Did Emmett get Uncle Hazard to get the cake? Probably he didn't, but Emmett's not one to turn down food, even if it's delivered by a dog. The two of them stroll off together munching on cake like partners in crime.

At supper, Daddy says that Settlers Days is going to keep him right busy for a spell, but that all the connections he is making are sure to lead to more employment opportunity. He says he'll bring the cakes in for a raffle.

"Say, did any Nashville letters come for me today?" Daddy asks.

"No Daddy," Becksie tells him. "Just some bills with more red letters."

Daddy says, "Always gonna be bills. Expect we can pay any of them, Jessie?"

Mama says, "We'll pay one this month, another next, and we'll have to float some checks and hope they don't get cashed."

"How can a check float, Mama?" Louise wants to know, but nobody answers.

"Cakes smell good," Daddy says, clearly hoping to change the subject. "By the way, I looked in the mirror today and my hair is going gray again. I can't compete with these younger folks trying to bust into the music scene too. As a musician, I got to have a head of black hair. I'm not even thirty-five. Why should I have gray hair? Look like some old man. It ain't right."

Mama says, "I'll dye it for you after supper, Tom, as usual."

I decide right then that I will take a walk after supper, as the kitchen gets real crowded with Mama trying to dye Daddy's hair black and the kids all wanting to watch.

"I'd appreciate that, darling."

I expect Mama to bring up Uncle Hazard and the applesauce cake and the broken plate, but she doesn't say a word. Seems like she's too wore-out. She casts her gaze out toward the ridge of the mountains, the line between her eyes a little deeper. I reach for her hand and hold it, but her fingers are limp in mine. I squeeze them, but she don't seem to notice. Gentle taps her fork on the table in short, sharp raps.

Cyrus says, "Hey listen, Gentle's making the woodpecker sound." Sure enough, as Gentle taps her fork, we can hear the woodpecker knocking away in the spruce pine. The old woodpecker and Gentle keep time as if they're chatting together. Then Daddy gets the banjo and starts to pick. As if on cue, Becksie and Jitters clog together on the wood floor to the sound of Daddy's banjo, while Louise plays the spoons on her legs. I grab my guitar and strum along with Daddy, and even Emmett whips out his harmonica to add his sweet notes to the music. Mama looks at all of us as if we've gone crazy.

Caroline and Cyrus try to clog with Becksie and Jitters, but they don't have the footwork right yet, which makes them like to bust out laughing on the floor. Gentle's face is lit with smiles, and sure enough, Mama can't help but grin in spite of herself. Daddy walks over to her, still strumming the banjo, and kisses her on the neck. He starts in singing an old song about "mole in the ground" who wants to root down the mountain. Sometimes our house is filled up with so much love and happiness that a body can't hardly stand it. I wonder if that old woodpecker in the spruce pine knows what he started.

With all the music around the supper table, the words to another song find their way into my head, but I don't think I'll be singing this one out loud anytime soon.

Mama floats a check to the landlord . . .
and another to the grocer in the valley.
Sometimes I think of all those floating checks . . .
flying high like birds on big white wings.
Will they bounce in the bank?
Or fly all the way to Mars?
Mama's real good at floating checks. . . .

After supper, Mama gets out the jar of black hair dye to make Daddy more competitive amongst the younger musicians, and I take off with my book of e.e. cummings poems. But first, I sneak out into the driveway over to Grandma's Chevy where I know Daddy will have a chocolate bar stashed in the glove compartment. That's where he keeps his secret chocolate. I open the glove compartment and sure enough, there it is. I grab the Hershey's bar and head up into the field of tall grass and sunflowers. I whistle for Uncle Hazard, who rests his head on my belly as I get settled with my book and chocolate. I aim to figure out how e.e. cummings strung all them words together in little poems. I read one about how "spring is like a perhaps hand" fixing everything up so pretty. I read another about some Cambridge ladies and how "the moon rattles like a fragment of angry candy." That one gives me tingles on the back of my neck.

Then I hear Mama and Daddy calling for me to come inside, but I want to keep reading my poems until it gets dark. "Livy Two! Livy Two!" I don't want to go back down to the house to help wash the babies or do the dishes. I cram the last of the chocolate bar into my mouth, letting the creamy sweetness melt on my tongue. Lord, it's good. Mama never buys chocolate. Never. I roll deeper into the field of sunflowers. I hear the front door slam, and I realize that Daddy's footsteps are getting closer. Through the stalks of sunflowers, I see him striding straight toward me with a towel around his neck, his hair dripping with black dye. It makes me nervous to see Daddy's face and ears dripping with black dye, like some crazy pirate. "Livy Two! Livy Two!" I burrow down deeper in the tall grass, playing possum, holding on to my e.e. cummings and tasting the last bits of chocolate in my mouth. He don't find me. Nobody ever does. Not in my secret places.

CHAPTER SIX

Watermelon Shoes

Early the next morning, a peach glow of sunrise casts itself around the holler. I look out my window and I see Daddy with his new head of black hair all thick and shiny, trying to sneak Uncle Hazard into Grandma Horace's car. For a second, I think I am still dreaming, but then I realize I am wide awake. Before he can drive off, I climb out the window and shimmy down the red maple as fast as I can and beat it out to the car.

"No sir!" I bang on the passenger window. In the backseat, I see four cakes ready to go for Settlers Days. "You cain't take him, Daddy. It's not just for me. It's Emmett. I'll hide the dog from Mama, but if you take him . . ."

Daddy reaches over and rolls down the window. "I hate to do it, Magnolia Blossom, but your Mama says I got to, so—"

Before he can utter another word, I reach inside the passenger seat and grab up Uncle Hazard like a football under my arm and take off like the wind. I'm faster than Daddy by a mile, and I sprint way past the pinecone palace deep into the woods and up the mountain path. I'm not letting my and Emmett's dog go. Heck, Louise hasn't even had a chance to paint a picture of him yet. I hide with Uncle Hazard in a patch of lilac bushes, my heart walloping behind my ribs. We wait for what seems like hours. Uncle Hazard pants with excitement at this new game, but Daddy doesn't come fetch him after all. From far away, I hear Grandma Horace's car start, and, from the way it coughs, I can tell it's still spitting black smoke. Daddy winds down the holler in the rattling Chevy.

I know I will get into a peck of trouble, but I don't care. This is my third day of having a dog, and though I'm trying not to like him much, I can't help it. Uncle Hazard looks at you and wags his tail as if to say, "Well, come on! What's next?" and it's hard not to feel excited about the day.

As I sneak down the trail to the creek, I place Uncle Hazard back in his pinecone palace and say, "You stay put, Uncle Hazard, or there will be hell to pay. I gotta go back and have breakfast, but you need to stay here, boy. It's the only way, you hear me?" He looks at me as if he understands and settles down good as gold. My nightgown is wet with dew, and my feet are grassy and muddy, but I feel strong and wide-awake.

For breakfast, Mama lets us eat the hunk of applesauce cake for Settlers Days that Uncle Hazard didn't steal. We wash the sweet crumbs down with buttermilk. The coffee smells good, especially with the lump of chicory Mama puts in it, and I sure wish I liked the taste, but I do not. From far away, I begin to hear the choking muffler sound coming back into the holler, and I wonder why Daddy is headed home so soon. Is it to get Uncle Hazard? I pray the dog has got the sense to stay hid in the pinecone palace.

Mama looks out the window. "What is your daddy up to?" She sighs and shakes her head. Then she looks at me. "By the way, Livy Two, where'd you take off to so fired-up early this morning?" Mama pushes the hair out of my eyes.

"No place." I keep my mouth full of cake so as not to have to answer more questions.

"Is that so? Well, you need to keep an eye on

Gentle in the garden today. I got more cakes to bake and some apple butter that needs putting up." Mama sniffs the air. "Do I smell rain coming? Well, we gotta get to work, rain or not."

"Yes, Mama," I say, relieved she doesn't ask about Uncle Hazard.

As her hands go a mile a minute, slapping our breakfast on the table, wiping crumbs from faces, Caroline watches her with a dreamy expression on her face. Then, out of the blue, Caroline asks, "Mama? If you blow up quicksand is it still quicksand?"

We all laugh, because Caroline always comes up with something peculiar to ask, but Mama shushes us and tells her, "Good Lord, eat your breakfast, child. I wouldn't know the first thing about it."

She slips Appelonia into a baby sack on her chest, and gets ready to start baking the two coconut cakes for a cakewalk contest at Settlers Days. Becksie and Jitters are already cracking eggs into the batter. Then I hear Daddy come inside, and my heart beats fast because I'm sure he's about to tell me to go get Uncle Hazard, but he doesn't so much as bother to look my way as he appears in the kitchen.

"Why are you back so soon, Tom?" Mama asks. "Mama's car okay?"

"It's fine. Can't forget my banjo! Gonna lose my

head one of these days," Daddy stops and looks at us all eating breakfast around the table. He grabs his banjo from the corner. "Lord Jessie, we got us a passel of fine-looking children, don't we?"

"They'll do. Don't forget that dog neither," Mama says. "A promise is a promise, Tom."

But Daddy just stands there grinning down at us, and his face looks so happy that I want to freeze it in my mind. He grabs up Gentle and nuzzles his face in her neck. "This child smells like sun and honeysuckle." He gets down eye-level to Cyrus and says, "Put up your dukes, son!" Giggling, Cyrus fake-punches Daddy in a "jab, jab, right cross" boxing match. "Who's tough now? Who's tough?"

"Me!" Cyrus acts more like a big boy every day. Next, Daddy swoops up Caroline into his arms and says, "Darling, you give your Daddy some kisses for the road." Caroline obliges him with sticky cake kisses. She says, "I love you so much I can't take it, Daddy." We all laugh. She's one for saying funny things like that.

Daddy says, "Look at the time. Lord, I better get on my way. Every clogger, fiddler, whittler, whistler, doll-maker, harmonica player, and picker is gonna be crawling out of these mountains today to show me their talent. Wish me luck, children." He grabs Mama around the waist and clogs with her around the kitchen.

"Can I go with you, Daddy?" Emmett puts his hand on Daddy's arm. "Please?"

"Not today, son. Another time." Daddy heads toward the door, but Emmett yells, "You always say that and there never is another time. I could help you."

Daddy studies Emmett, and I pray for him to say yes, just once. "You won't get in a fight with the Buck Mountain boys, even if they try to rub poison ivy on you again?"

"I swear." Emmett stands tall. "And I could take notes. Tell you who's good and who's not worth a lick. Livy Two can handle things here. She's tough as any boy."

I feel a blush creep onto my face, but I sit up proud and straight.

"You don't have to tell me that, son." Daddy tugs my braids.

"So please?" Emmett asks. "I could even help you write your hit banjo song in between auditions. All you need is a good manager, a businessman, and I am sure—"

Daddy says, "Emmett, you could talk a poll-parrot into an early grave. I think a lawyer is the profession for you. Get in the car then." He turns to the rest of us.

"You'uns, get out in the garden and do what needs doing." Daddy kisses Mama and says, "Lord, I got the prettiest wife that ever did take a breath of air." He heads out of the house and climbs in Grandma Horace's car where Emmett waits. As they drive off, I see where he has taken a coat hanger and wired an orange juice can over a hole in the muffler. That's Daddy's favorite trick for a contrary muffler. I surely hope Uncle Hazard stays put in his pinecone palace, or else Mama will know Daddy broke his promise even though it wasn't his fault.

It's another hot July morning, and nobody much wants to be weeding and watering, but we got to if we want to save any of the vegetables. Cracking summer rainstorms have already washed out the garden twice, so we've had to replant everything a couple times. Probably won't have much of a harvest anyway, according to Mama, but something is better than nothing. Our summer garden is in the shape of a gigantic tomato. Daddy designed it and said that there was no divine law on God's green earth that said a garden could only be square. The garden could be a circle if we had a mind to make it so, and we did, planting everything from collard greens to mustard greens to beans to squash to sweet potatoes to Irish potatoes to corn to spinach to carrots to bush beans to pole beans to I can't remember what else.

We always order our seeds from the Burpee's catalog. I love to look at the seed catalog with the different greens, reds, oranges, and purples of all the vegetables. We don't order flower seeds, as we got more than a hundred kinds of wildflowers growing all around Maggie Valley. My favorite wild mountain flower is a jack-in-the-pulpit because it grows near waterfalls. The jack-in-the-pulpit flower has three leaves sticking out of its stalk, and in the middle of the flower, it looks like a preacher man giving a talk.

I sit down with Gentle on my lap near where the twins are building a city with orange juice cans, a ball of string, twigs, and matchbox cars. Cyrus can't tie the strings around the twigs very well, so Caroline is trying to help him. She wears a pair of large paper wings on her back, and says to Cyrus, "I am a mountain fairy, and if you're very good, I will grant your wish and help you build your fair city."

"Just hurry up and tie it, fairy," Cyrus says as he makes a tall building with orange juice cans.

Daddy brought home some cans of frozen orange juice from Cas Walker's store, but they melted in the car. Mama refroze them, but the juice tasted funny.

Gentle squirms down off my lap to wiggle her toes in a patch of violets. She is getting fast on her feet, though I know she can't see so good because of the way she knocks into things. She sniffs the air the same way Uncle Hazard does when something strikes his fancy—like now, the way she leans over and breathes in the violets. I show her how to strum my guitar. She cocks her head as if listening real hard for something. She feels around for my guitar and rubs her fingers over the strings. It's like she peeks at life with her ears and fingers.

Late last night when they thought we were asleep, I heard Mama ask Daddy again about Gentle's eyes, but Daddy snapped at her. "All our children are healthy, Jessie. No doctor is gonna say any different. I wouldn't pay two bits to some old doctor."

"You don't have two bits to pay."

"All I'm saying—"

"I know what you're saying, but we can't ignore it either. Tom. Tom?"

But Daddy was already picking at his banjo, so he didn't have to listen. Yet, sometimes, he sets Gentle on his knee and peers into her eyes as if seeking answers. I seen it for myself. Lord knows, we don't got the money for a doctor, but I know Mama would like to go anyway, just to talk to somebody who wouldn't bite her head off for asking. Mama always goes to the hospital to have her babies, but we don't go to the doctor much ourselves. And it's true, we're hardly ever sick except for when we all got the measles a long time ago. When we get earaches, Mama uses warm olive oil and a rag to coax out the pain. She makes a garlic and onion salve for our chests when we get colds, and she gives us warm mint tea for coughs. Mama believes in going to the doctors if it's real bad, but what with money being so scarce, she don't see no sense in paying someone to diagnose what she can fix with a homemade remedy. Daddy says he don't trust doctors as far as he can throw them.

Cyrus starts to cry when Caroline, still pretending to be a fairy, skips over Cyrus's part of the dirt city, knocking over twigs and string.

"Hang on," I say. "I can fix it." I tie the string back to the twigs in a flash and stand the twigs upright again like baby telephone poles in the dirt. "This here is the electricity that goes from pole to pole and gives folks light in their houses. Daddy didn't have electricity when he was growing up in the country, but Mama did because she comes from city folk."

Then Caroline pirouettes like a real ballerina and asks, "Is it tomorrow yet?"

I say, "Not yet, and you got to be careful about

jumping on the city, Caroline," but she's already back to leaping around the edges of the garden, calling, "I'm a mountain fairy! Can't catch me."

Louise shouts, "Hey, you'uns want to see the kind of shoes Daddy wore as a country boy?" Louise jumps up and shows us her feet. That girl has done gone and tied shoelaces around old watermelon rinds, which she wears on her bare feet.

"Where'd you get them?" Becksie demands. "Mama likes to pickle the rinds."

"Aw, the Mennonites threw them out. Lookee here," Louise laughs. "Watermelon shoes. The exact kind Daddy wore as a boy." Then she talks in an old scratchy voice like she was ninety years old or something, and says, "Listen you'uns, we was too poor for regular shoes, that's the truth, but watermelon shoes worked fine."

"We want watermelon shoes!" Caroline and Cyrus jump up and down.

"Course you'uns do. Don't you know every dadgummed member of Daddy's whole family had a pair of watermelon shoes? Why the ladies even carved heels into the rinds so they could look hoity-toity when they went to church."

Becksie says, "Louise, you know you're just making that up."

"That's right!" Jitters squirts tomato seeds through her teeth as she talks.

Louise looks around and winks, "I do believe there is one big echo in this holler." With that, she grabs up Jitters, who starts whooping, but I can see her secret laughter.

"Put me down!" Jitters shouts as I sing a silly song that pops into my head.

> *"Watermelon shoes for sale!*
> *Get your high heels, your low heels, your no heels!*
> *Latest style, latest trend . . .*
> *if you want folks to think you're in . . .*
> *get your watermelon shoes for sale!"*

"Hey, maybe I ought to audition for Mr. Cas Walker," I say, but the sound of a truck coming up into the holler makes us all stop and look toward the grinding gears. Mathew the Mennonite is back, but why? Louise sees him and ducks behind the smokehouse. It's funny how she can be real silly and cut-up with us one minute, but go silent as the grave the very next when a stranger or even a neighbor comes into the holler. We watch real careful as Mathew the Mennonite pulls to a stop. Then who should he help out of his black truck but our grandmother, the witch herself from Enka-Stinka. I'd of recognized her anywhere from the picture on Mama's nightstand. Grandma Horace looks fired-up mad. She swats the air around Mathew the Mennonite as if he were an irksome fly.

"Be careful, young man. This is a new dress from the Sears and Roebuck catalog," Grandma Horace snaps, but if that old lady knew anything, she would not brag about her new doodad dress from the Sears & Roebuck catalog. The Mennonites don't care a fiddle about store-bought nothing. I want to yell at Grandma Horace to be sweet to Mathew the Mennonite, who would be a shy man whether he was a Mennonite or not.

"Here's your quarter for driving me from the bus station." Grandma digs around in her purse for a quarter. "Thank you, sir."

Mathew the Mennonite takes the quarter. Mama comes out of the house, and when she lays her eyes on Grandma Horace, she breaks into a wide smile. The two women run together—they're so happy to see each other again after what must be four or five years. It's like they was never even mad in the first place. When Mama gets done hugging on Grandma Horace, she turns to Mathew the Mennonite and says, "Thank you for bringing my mama, Mr. Mathew. Would you like to come inside and set a spell?"

"No ma'am," Mr. Mathew says. "I must be on my way."

Grandma Horace gazes at us through her good eye,

and even her glass one doesn't seem to miss much. "Growing like weeds. And just look at the new ones. Lord Jessie, how many are y'all going to have?"

Mama says, "Well Mama, you know Tom was raised a Catholic. They believe God never sends more children than you can care for."

"I didn't think your Tom attended church, Catholic or otherwise."

"Well, that's a different chapter to the story," Mama says, but Grandma Horace is aiming for a closer inspection, and from the look on her face, she ain't real thrilled with what she sees. She asks, "How are y'all? I see faces that could use some soap and water."

We all shout, "Fine," and then I add, "Hey, look at Louise's watermelon shoes."

Louise shakes a foot into the air from behind the smokehouse, but nothing more. Grandma Horace gives us a sorry look and goes into the house with Mama. Mathew the Mennonite says, "You know, I don't believe I've ever seen a pair of watermelon shoes."

"Ain't they something?" I say. "Show him the other one, Louise."

Louise obliges with the other foot, but keeps well hidden. Mathew the Mennonite says, "They surely are something indeed. You folks take care now." He tips his straw hat and gets in his black truck to drive back out of the holler. As we all wave, I reach to pick up Gentle to have her wave too, but she isn't beside me anymore. I glance around but I can't see her anywhere, and my heart leaps into my mouth. In all the confusion of the watermelon shoes and Grandma Horace arriving, I've lost her.

CHAPTER SEVEN

Lost

She was just here a minute ago, or was it five? Or ten? I start calling and calling for her, and Mama bolts out of the house, all the blood drained from her face. "I told you to watch her, Livy Two. You promised me!"

"I was watching her," I cry, and then we all take off, calling, "Gentle, Gentle!" Nobody argues about who goes where or does what. We all just run like the dickens to find our sister who's crawled off somewhere in the holler. From off in the distance, I hear a clap of thunder and it makes me run even faster. I whisper a prayer to the first Livy buried on Black Mountain: "Please Livy One, wherever you are, watch out for Gentle. She's just a little thing.

Please keep an eye on Gentle and help us find her quick."

As I race through the holler with Louise at my side, the branches of the pines and poplars scratch at the clouds in the hot summer breeze. Raindrops pelt my face.

"She couldn't a got far, Livy Two," Louise yells, her voice ragged, as she catches up to me, watermelon shoes long gone.

I can't even answer her I am so scared. For a split second, I think for sure I'll lose my breakfast of cake and buttermilk, but I will the food to stay in my stomach. There are things to beware of in these mountains— things like copperheads, cottonmouths, rattlesnakes, and even hornets' nests. Gentle doesn't know of these wild creatures and varmints. How could she? She's not even three years old. She could crawl right on one and never see a thing.

Louise speaks in gasping breaths. "It's not your fault, Livy Two. It's not. We were all supposed to be watching."

I still don't answer. I don't got nothing to say. It is my fault. It is my job to watch Gentle. I did wrong, and so I can't listen to words of comfort with the sky leaking rain and the sun fighting to get out. *Where is Gentle?* My question becomes a kind of chant.

Gentle, where are you baby?
Gentle, please answer me true. . . .
Gentle, you are my sweetheart. . . .
Gentle, I'm coming for you. . . .

I race toward the creek, terrified of what I might see, but it's only cool water racing over the smooth stones. I call her name over and over again. Silence except for a mad scramble of blue jays and squirrels in the treetops and the sleepy sound of cicadas and tree frogs, buzzing, buzzing, buzzing like a hacksaw nightmare in my brain. I look far down into sloping fields that lead to Mathew the Mennonite's holler. Nothing. Where could she have got to? My heart is a brick in my chest, and with each step, my feet feel like they're sinking deeper and deeper into quicksand. I can't run fast enough. Is this a dream? Let it be a dream. I've never lost anyone. Mama trusted me.

I hear Louise behind me, calling, "Gentle, where are you, girl? Where are you? Gentle!" In another part of the holler, I hear Becksie and Jitters calling too. It's too long . . . it's been too long.

As I go around the flat rock that leads to another section of the creek, I come upon a sight that makes me go weak at the knees. Louise stops short when she sees it too. Gentle teeters on the edge of the bank where the water rushes wide and deep, ready to topple in at any second. But each time she slips closer to the creek, Uncle Hazard races back and forth in front of her, barking his head off. Gentle laughs wildly at this game, but then I hear a scream. I turn to see Mama racing toward the creek, but she stops suddenly when she spies Uncle Hazard wrangling Gentle. Then, just as Gentle steps forward again toward the water, Uncle Hazard jumps up and knocks her backward onto a bed of Queen Anne's lace.

Gentle's laughter echoes through the holler as butterflies swirl above her hands and face. She shrieks with delight when Uncle Hazard begins licking her face in the light sprinkle of rain. His rough tongue tickles her nose, and he shakes the water off of his coat, spraying droplets everywhere. She grabs his collar and rolls over on top of him. He peeks out from under her stomach and waits patiently as she inspects his eyes, ears, and nose with her busy fingers. Uncle Hazard nuzzles his head on her lap as if he's protecting her, and Gentle tugs on his floppy ears.

As we rush toward her, Uncle Hazard leaps up barking like a wild thing, her fierce protector, but then he sees it's only us and settles down again on Gentle's lap. Something breaks in me, and I fall to my knees and start throwing up. I can't help it. My stomach ain't my own no more. My baby sister is okay, but I can't quite believe it.

When I'm done getting sick and can breathe again, Louise lets me cry and pats me on the back. Then Mama helps me to the creek where I wash my face and mouth. We all keep an eye on Gentle the whole time.

"What are you'uns doing?" Two familiar voices yelp, as Becksie and Jitters appear over the hill and stare down at Gentle and Uncle Hazard. Becksie points and shouts, "Lord, you found her. Good thing. And look at that there dog. You know you'uns aren't supposed to keep it, right Mama?"

Jitters echoes, "You're gonna catch it, Livy Two, right Mama? Right?"

Mama only says, "Hush." Then she gathers up Gentle in her arms and inhales all the air around her baby girl's head. She looks down at Uncle Hazard and says, "I'm much obliged to you, dog. I seen what you did, and I thank you."

Uncle Hazard thumps his tail at Mama and rises up on his back haunches into the shape of a question mark. "Is that a trick you aim to show me, sir?" Mama asks.

But with all this attention from Mama, Uncle Hazard gets so excited he tips over backward. Shaking himself off, he sits up again into a begging question mark just waiting to see what Mama will say.

"Mama," Louise whispers, "Uncle Hazard wants to stay."

"Is that a fact?" Mama inspects Uncle Hazard.

Becksie cocks her head. "Ain't you mad as the dickens, Mama?"

"Mad, mad, mad." Jitters hops about, hoping for the explosion.

"That's enough," Mama says in a low voice as sweet as silk and honey. "Anyhow, I'm not mad. It all just drained out of me. Now I'm . . ."

"Happy?" asks Caroline.

"Of course, she's happy," Cyrus says. "We done found Gentle. Right Mama?"

"That's right, son," Mama agrees. "That's right."

With that, Gentle laces her fingers around Mama's neck like a little spider monkey. I can see that Mama would like to bust out crying with relief, but I know she's holding it inside. Mama never cries except around Livy One's birthday and death day, which are one and the same. She cries in her room at night on that anniversary. I always hear Daddy comfort her, talking about the strong healthy children they still have. Once, I heard Mama say that she didn't believe in grown-ups crying in front of children, getting them all worked up and afraid. But I wouldn't be afraid of Mama's tears.

After a few moments of all of us just touching Gentle, patting her like she's a puppy herself, Jitters asks the question we all been thinking. "But Mama, what about Uncle Hazard? You said we couldn't—"

"Would you zip it for longer than one single second?" I elbow Jitters.

And by some miracle, she does. There is a long silence as Mama looks good and hard at Uncle Hazard whose ears go flat with worry. Finally, Mama says, "I reckon, this dog saved my girl and my heart today. The dog stays. Might as well bring him up from the creek. Fix him up a place near the house. Not inside. Just near, you hear me?"

We all start yelling and hollering. Uncle Hazard barks and rolls over on his back. A half-lemon sun pushes out of the clouds.

"Mama," I begin, "I'm real sorry. It was my fault."

Mama touches my face and says, "Livy Two, I seen the way you love this girl. Now, I put a lot on you kids, and I don't blame you for losing track. But we got to be a whole lot more careful. All of us. I know I haven't said it much, but this girl can't see so good yet. So we gotta be her eyes. Maybe this dog can help too."

"Yes, Mama." I lean into her, hot tears pricking

my own eyes. I pick up Caroline, and Louise grabs up Cyrus on her shoulders, and we all follow Mama up to the house where Grandma Horace stands alert on the front porch, holding baby Appelonia and my guitar. She don't look none too pleased at getting left out of the excitement.

Before we reach the porch, Grandma Horace barks, "Well, look at the kit and caboodle of y'all, traipsing out in the rain like a pack of wild animals. And Olivia Hyatt Weems, I rescued your guitar out of the garden, thank you very much. Seems to me a big girl like you would know to get a guitar out of the rain."

"Thank you, Grandma Horace." I take the guitar from the witch. "By the way, Gentle is just fine in case you were wondering. She didn't get attacked by a bear or bit by a copperhead."

"Livy Two!" Mama's voice carries a low warning note.

"Well, she could act like she cares, Mama," I say right back.

Grandma Horace fixes her good eye on me. "I've got a nice cake of soap in my grip, and I'll use it to wash out smart mouths. See if I won't, young lady."

I eye the witch, who strokes the mole on her upper lip with a fat finger. She says, "In my day, girls didn't go around picking on guitars. Wasn't fitten."

"Yeah, we'll have to work on making Livy Two fitten," Louise giggles and pulls stickweeds out of my hair.

"That'll be the day," says Becksie. "Ha!"

"Yep," Jitters nods. "That'll be the day. Ha!"

Louise pipes up, "That's a real pretty dress you're wearing, Grandma Horace." For some reason, Louise ain't afraid of Grandma, but that old lady scares me like nobody's business.

Grandma Horace says, "Don't think about buttering me up, Miss Louise Weems. I am not one to be buttered up." She sets Appelonia in the bassinet on the porch. "Hello Rebecca, Myrtle-Anne. Well, don't those dresses from the church bazaar look fine on you two."

"Thank you, Grandma Horace." Becksie curtsies.

"Yes, thank you," Jitters says with a curtsy too, only she trips and falls, but Grandma Horace is already casting her good eye toward the rest of us. "Too bad the others look like something the cat dragged in, if nobody minds my saying so."

"I do mind," Mama says. "There's no need to be spiteful, Mama."

"Why, I'm not being spiteful," Grandma says. "I'm speaking the truth. You know I have always spoken the truth. Folks just have to accept that, but Lord, look at you, Jessie. You look plain awful. Where's my pretty child? So many babies wearing you out. I didn't raise my daughter to be a cow, giving birth year after year."

"That's enough!" Mama speaks in an ice-cold voice I've not heard before, but Grandma Horace isn't finished. "Where is that husband you married? And where is my Chevrolet? Lord, don't y'all bother to offer your guests a glass of sweet iced tea?" Grandma Horace puts her hand on her broad hip.

"We're fresh out of iced tea. One of you go get your grandmother some water," Mama says, and so Becksie runs off to fetch a glass of water. When she comes back, Grandma Horace takes the glass and drinks it down in one swallow. "Thank you, Rebecca."

"Her name is Becksie," Jitters reminds Grandma Horace, but she isn't listening.

Grandma Horace shifts back to look at Mama. "Jessie, I am only surprised you haven't lost more children living up in these piney woods the way y'all do. They could get off to just about anyplace. I don't see why y'all don't move back to Enka with me and go to school in a little town. It's crazy living up here. After all, it's the nineteen-sixties. The age of civilization for most sensible folk." Grandma's glass eye glints in the sun as she folds her arms across her bosom and settles herself into a rocker on the front porch.

Mama says, "There's a real good school in Maggie Valley. The kids just finished up in May. They'll go back again in the fall."

"Can't be as good as the ones in Enka or Asheville. Do they shove all ages into one classroom like the old days? I expect they do." Grandma Horace acts like she knows everything there is to know about all the schools in North Carolina. But Mama don't answer. She grew up in Enka-Stinka and has no desire to be rushing back to her girlhood town. Mama says the mountains are her home now. She kisses Gentle and picks up her knitting out of the basket on the porch. The silver needles flash out of the red and purple yarn with Mama's flying fingers. She starts humming a song called "Good Ole Mountain Dew." Uncle Hazard must like that old tune, for he scrambles up onto the porch and leaps onto Grandma Horace's big lap with a happy "howdy there" pant.

Grandma Horace gives him a piercing stare, which makes him slink down her legs to the porch, his toenails clicking across the wood. Uncle Hazard has a lot to learn. None of us grandchildren would ever dare to climb into Grandma Horace's lap. There are just some things you do not attempt in this life.

"A dog too?" Grandma Horace asks. "What's next?"

"His name is Uncle Hazard." Becksie smoothes out her apron.

"We aim to keep him," Jitters adds.

"Daddy says he came from Hazard, Kentucky." Louise heads back to her canvas, paintbrushes bobbing in her back pocket. "He rescued Gentle just now from drowning."

"Is that a fact?" Grandma Horace says, as if she don't believe a word of it. "Well, aside from the acquisition of a dog being pure foolishness, I got one more thing to say," Grandma Horace directs her attention to Gentle. "If I'm not mistaken, that child hasn't looked at me once. Surely, she needs an eye doctor. Hear me, daughter? I'll make the appointment myself."

I've heard all I can stand for one day. I grab my guitar and leap off the porch and head off to the fields. I whistle for Uncle Hazard who follows me down the path. The green is so thick around me I feel like I'm in a jungle. There are splashes of pink from the lady's-slippers growing on the river's edge. I don't know why I'm so scared of Grandma Horace's words when I've asked the very same thing myself. But it's all just too much. Gentle getting lost, the witch appearing and telling us everything that's wrong with us. I find a stump and pick out a few chords on my guitar.

Gentle serenades the flowers
that bloom after the showers
that rain down in Maggie Valley.

Under a canopy of mountains
Gentle plays in all the fountains
that burst up in Maggie Valley.

Pretty soon, I hear Louise carrying Gentle through the edge of the woods, telling her all about color. "Now Gentle, eat this blueberry and you'll understand the color blue. Azure, sapphire, navy, and indigo. That's other names for blue." I get real quiet so they don't know I'm nearby. I just want to hear Louise talk to Gentle. Next, she matter-of-factly lists all the shades of green: "Green means emerald, olive, aqua, and forest. Feel these leaves. Smell the pines and moss. You smell all that? That's green, little gal."

"Green, Louise?" Gentle repeats.

Then Louise says, "Red: cardinal, crimson, russet, and scarlet. Think of the oven in the kitchen when the blast of hot air hits you in face."

"Mama's biscuits?"

Louise says, "That's right. Okay, next is yellow: golden, honey, canary yellow, amber, and saffron. Think of sun on your face and honey on your bread and that's yellow. Purple: lilac, lavender, orchid, plum, and violet. Remember the coolness in the air before it rains. Remember, Gentle?"

I close my eyes and drift into Louise's words, and soon I am inside one of my sister's paintings, part of the color, light, and shadow. Another song eases into my head as I listen to my sisters talking colors.

If I told you that blue meant indigo
if I told you that yellow meant gold
if I told you that red meant crimson
would you see the colors that I know?

CHAPTER EIGHT

Ring of Seven Sisters

As the sun slants across the afternoon sky, me and Louise take apart the sticks, pinecones, and redbud leaves of Uncle Hazard's pinecone palace. We rebuild it by the side of our house and find some old boards and plywood under the house to make it much sturdier and stronger. Daddy and Emmett are not yet home from choosing talent at Settlers Days and we want to surprise them. Mama still don't know how we're going to afford to feed Uncle Hazard, but I decide to start thinking up ways to earn money myself. I wonder how much sacks of dog food cost down in Maggie Valley.

We glue more pinecones to the roof with some sticky sorghum and cut out a window with Emmett's carving knife. Louise wants to build a winding staircase out of more pinecones for Uncle Hazard's palace, which is just fine, but Becksie and Jitters want to paint it pink. Pink! The last thing Uncle Hazard needs is a dadgummed pink pinecone palace, but I tell them they can make him some pink curtains if they got their hearts dead set on it, and they gallop into the house all excited to start sewing.

About every other second, I have to chase the twins away from Uncle Hazard's new home, cause all they want to do is knock it over. I teach them how to make a path of rocks leading up to the door of the pinecone palace. Gentle helps gather stones too, but Mama keeps coming out the door every five seconds to make sure Gentle is still with us. "I'm watching her, I done told you, I am," I say.

Mama replies, "I'm checking on all my children."

Once we're done, Mama comes out to study our masterpiece and declares, "That's the prettiest dog-house I've ever seen in my whole life."

"Pinecone palace," Gentle insists.

The twins tightrope-walk the fence around the pinecone palace. Cyrus yells, "Can I sleep with Uncle Hazard tonight?"

"Me too!" Caroline says. "We want to sleep with Uncle Hazard in his beautiful pinecone palace."

I feel real proud, but then Grandma Horace looks at

us with a sour lime face and remarks, "No grandchildren are gonna be sleeping out in any doghouse."

"It ain't no doghouse, Grandma Horace. It's a pinecone palace," I explain in my most polite voice.

"Call it what you want," the old lady replies, "but if you ask my candid opinion, that get-up is a lot of foolishness for a dog."

Louise mutters under her breath, "I don't believe anyone did ask for your candid opinion."

Grandma Horace says, "I heard that." But she just keeps rocking away on one of the white rockers on the porch.

"Hey," I say, "we truly ought to celebrate finding Gentle. Let's go on over to Ghost Town in the Sky. Let's pretend we're rich folks all the way from New York City come down to the mountains for a day. We could take Uncle Hazard with us. Heck, I bet this dog would love to ride a chairlift up and over the mountain. Ears flapping in the wind like sails. Emmett would love it too."

"Could we, Mama?" Louise hangs up the sign "Uncle Hazard's Pinecone Palace."

"No money for that kind of foolishness," Mama says. "You'uns ought to know that by now." Then she pulls me to her and says, "But Livy Two, I have hatched a plan." She removes a rope from her apron pocket and proceeds to tie Gentle to me with a long rope. One end is around my waist, and the other end is around Gentle.

At first, I think she's fooling with me and playing a joke. I say, "Aw Mama, you don't have to tie us together. I told you I won't lose her again." But Mama doesn't answer. She just makes expert knots on the ropes around our waists.

"Mama, please. I said I'd be careful. It's not funny," I say.

But it's like Mama has gone deaf. Grandma Horace sits up straight as a board. "Child's right, Jessie. You can't be tying those children together."

"Mama, this is my business. Leave off."

"I'm saying it's not right." Grandma Horace stands up and goes over to Mama.

Louise looks at us from where she's putting the finishing touches on the pinecone palace staircase, her face sad. Even Becksie and Jitters keep quiet from their perch in the kitchen window, but they're watching too, right along with the twins.

"Mama, I don't want to be tied up." A sob rises in my throat. I try to swallow it back down. I know Mama's still scared about today, but I swear, sometimes, I already feel like I got all these invisible ropes tied to me with everybody needing or wanting something from me. *Can you keep a secret, Livy Two? Livy Two, clean up the babies. Livy Two, mind Gentle! Livy Two! Livy Two!* This real rope makes me feel like I'm strangling. How am I ever going to cut loose and be free to sail the Mississippi River or climb the Great Wall of China if I'm tethered to the holler in this way? "Mama? I don't want this rope. Please?"

But Mama doesn't answer as she takes a basket of sheets to the clothesline and hangs them out to dry. Seeing Mama's pretty face all streaked with worry, I know she's panicky and not thinking straight. I glance at Gentle, who plays with the rope around her waist. Already she thinks it's a game. I let her tug at me, and I tug back to make her laugh.

Mama says, "Keep the rope on. I mean it."

Appelonia starts to wail from the house, so Mama goes inside to tend to her. I yank at the rope around my waist, but Mama's tied it good and tight. I can't undo the knot. I look over at Gentle's hair spilling down her back, and suddenly, I know that Livy One has the very same yellow waterfall hair up in heaven. I don't rightly know why, but somehow Gentle and Livy One are connected in my mind. Gentle listens to me more than anyone in this loud-talking family, and so does Livy One when I offer up my prayers and worries to her. I hope to see Livy One's grave one day on Black Mountain, and

I try to picture that day to take my mind off the rope. I will bring my dead sister daisies, wild geraniums, and sweet white violets to make a bed of flowers around her headstone.

As I fiddle with the rope some more, Grandma Horace comes over with a pair of scissors and cuts us loose. She doesn't say a word about it, but when she's done, she takes the rope and tosses it in the trash can behind the house. I gather Gentle on my lap and sing a song about sister ties.

> *There's a ring of seven sisters in the sky.*
> *There's a ring of seven sisters in the sky.*
> *All tied together that ring of seven sisters*
> *a sparkly rope looping seven hearts*
> *a way up high. . . .*

CHAPTER NINE

Venus

When the Big Dipper dots the indigo night sky, Emmett and Daddy finally wheeze back into the holler from Settlers Days tryouts. Now Grandma's car makes a new clang-clang rattle along with the choking sound. I hear Emmett say, "We ought to get that looked at, Daddy," as they get out of the car, but Daddy don't seem to hear that advice. Instead, he plops down on the porch swing and announces, "I'm here to tell you, we saw a heap of worthy and peculiar talent."

"Did we ever!" Emmett chimes in. "My favorite was the cloggin' doll-maker."

Daddy says. "I cain't hardly think of it no more. Now one of you'uns go bring your daddy a tall glass of spring water and a cool rag for my pounding head. I need to make me a pan of roasted peanuts, and then all will be right with the world."

Becksie says, "I'll get it," and runs to fetch him water.

Emmett says, "I'll get the peanuts started, Daddy. Then you can tell 'em all about your commercial."

"What commercial?" Louise says. "Did you get one?"

"Not a commercial yet. Don't count them chicks too fast. It's an audition," Daddy explains, "but it looks good. For shoes. Don't tell Mama. I want it to be a surprise. Here's what they want me to play." Daddy sings, "Don't be blue about your shoes. Come to the Shoe-Drop-In in Buncombe County and get ready to go high-stepping!"

Emmett says, "I helped him get it too. I got those boys to come over and talk to you, didn't I, Daddy? Didn't I?"

"That's right, son. You sure did."

Becksie says, "Hey, can you guess who's here to visit, Daddy?" She brings out two cups of cold water.

Jitters chimes in, "Yep, guess, Daddy, guess! Go on! But you never will!"

Daddy takes a cup of water. "Just a minute, darlings. Let your daddy catch his breath and have a cool drink."

"Me too," Emmett grins and gulps down the other cup.

I can tell Emmett has had a real good day with Daddy, and I'm glad for them, but before they can get too comfortable, I talk fast and low about Gentle getting lost in the holler and how Uncle Hazard found her at the edge of the creek. Nobody interrupts, not Emmett, Becksie, Jitters, nor Louise, who sit on the porch too.

"Where's that dog now?" Daddy asks.

Louise points and says, "Look yonder."

We all look and see Uncle Hazard snoring like a king in his pinecone palace. He doesn't look very dignified for a mountain rescue dog, but I'm still proud of him.

"One heck of a watchdog," Daddy shakes his head. "But I reckon he's tuckered."

Then Becksie says, "Livy Two, you forgot to say how Mama tied you and Gentle up together."

"That's right," says Jitters. "You forgot to say all about that."

I take a breath to keep my temper. "Why, you'uns just did tell him. Thank you, Queen Flapping-Jaws."

When I turn to Daddy, he says, "I need to do some talking to your mama, children. Would you pardon your daddy a moment?" As he opens the front door to find Mama, he runs smack into Grandma Horace, who demands, "Well, look here who showed his face. How's my car I come to claim, Tom Weems? Sounding mighty poorly from what I just heard crawl into this holler you call home. What's all this about a hanger and orange juice can parlaying as a muffler on my Chevrolet?"

"Howdy, Mother Horace. When did you arrive? You're looking healthy."

"Don't howdy-healthy me, boy."

"Now, Mother Horace, we'll talk. Indeed, we will talk," Daddy swerves around Grandma Horace like a high-speed locomotive. "But first I got to see to my wife and tell her I got a radio commercial audition for shoes first thing in the morning and hear about the excitement of her day."

As Daddy ducks into the room to see Mama, all of us gathered on the porch try not to laugh, but the giggles escape anyway. When Grandma Horace lights into Daddy, it's easy to picture him at age ten, shaking in his boots from a stern talking-to from a grown-up.

Then Emmett makes me tell him everything all over again from start to finish. After I do, down to the watermelon shoes and Uncle Hazard saving the day and my worry over Gentle's eyes, Emmett whistles and says, "Hold it. I got it, Livy. I got an idea."

"What?"

Emmett says, "Listening to you talk just now, it hit me how Uncle Hazard can help Gentle. He can be her Seeing Eye dog. They're the special dogs who help folks who can't see so good. I know he don't have no training, but maybe he could learn."

Louise jumps up and says, "Hey, I bet that Miss Attickson you like so much has a book about Seeing Eye dogs. When's the lending library truck due next?"

In that moment, I feel like I have the smartest brother and sister in the world. Why didn't I think of that myself?

Then Becksie says, "I don't know. Ain't they special dogs, Emmett? That dog ain't that special. He slobbers."

"Why do you have to act like that?" I yell at Becksie.

"Like what?" Becksie says. "Truthful? Too bad for you. He has strings of slobber when he shakes. Tell me he don't."

"Yep, strings of 'em," Jitters nods. "Sure does."

"You'uns act like Uncle Hazard is nothing," I cry, fed up with Becksie's spying and doubting and telling on me. "He might could help Gentle. He saved her life today."

Emmett speaks up, "Uncle Hazard is special. I could teach him. We all will."

Louise says, "That's right. Besides, we can't afford no real Seeing Eye dog."

"I just don't think you should git your hopes up is all," Becksie says.

"That's right." Jitters nods.

"It will work," I say. "It has to." I decide I'd better go down to the lending library and get the guide dog book myself from Miss Attickson first thing in the morning. I surely do hope she's due to arrive in Maggie Valley tomorrow.

But the next morning, Mama has other plans. She says we're going to take Gentle to get her eyes checked in Enka-Stinka by a real doctor who specializes in eyes. Everybody leaps up and begs to go, but Mama says, "No, just Livy Two." When the other kids start griping, Mama says, "Hush. Grandma Horace's poor car won't hold us all." Then she turns to me and says, "Wash your face and brush your teeth and scrub those scabby elbows, so the doctor won't think we're a bunch of hillbillies living all the way up here. And borrow Becksie's dress. The red gingham."

"I hate that Enka-Stinka dress. It won't fit anyway."

"Put it on now. I'm not fooling around."

Mama's tone could melt ice, so I know better than to argue too much. I stomp toward the closet to get the ugly dress, but I plead, "Fine, I'll wear it, but can we at least stop at the lending library truck, Mama? On the way?"

"Not today," Mama says. "Now go scrub yourself like I done told you, girl."

After I yank on the stupid dress and go back to the breakfast table, Madame Becksie gives me a black look. She does not like it at all that I get to go into town and wear her dress on top of it, so she says, "I'm the one who should be going, Mama. And I wouldn't lose track of Gentle neither with my head in the clouds over some new guitar song."

"Me neither," sniffs Jitters.

Before I can crack them a good one, Gentle says, "*No!* I want Livy Two."

I think better of slugging Becksie and Jitters, and I pull Gentle onto my lap. Grandma Horace appears all dressed up in another Sears & Roebuck catalog dress and lace-up black shoes. As she makes her way into the kitchen, she seems a little stunned by all the noise and crowding around the table. Today, instead of grits, Mama makes us one giant biscuit to share. Little Cyrus takes one look at it on the table and shouts, "Goddamn, what a biscuit!" Caroline claps her hand over her twin's mouth. "That's a bad word, Cyrus!"

Grandma Horace turns three shades of raspberry pink, and we all try not to laugh, but we can't help it.

Even Mama pinches her smile into a frown, but her eyes dance with laughter. Grandma Horace sucks down her hot coffee and says, "Aside from the pitiful manners at this table, this breakfast is a sorry sight, Jessie. How do you expect these children to grow up strong on a diet of biscuit slivers for breakfast?"

I guess Mama can't take no more of Grandma Horace's opinions, cause she pitches the empty biscuit skillet into the sink and says, "You listen to me, Mama. I was real happy to see you, but you ain't been up here a whole day after five whole years of not speaking to us, but still you know everything there is to know. I am doing the best that I can with all these kids, Mama, and all you do is pick, pick, pick. What else would you have me do? For lunch, the children will eat blackberries, butter beans with fatback, and sweet corn if it's ripe. We ain't starved yet."

"Well, not starved, exactly," Emmett says.

"You hush up, Emmett Weems!" Mama warns him.

"All I'm saying is that living the way you—" Grandma Horace begins, but Mama snaps, "I know what you're saying, Mama, and I need you to quit doling out the free advice. If this is going to work, you coming back into our lives, you need to quit. Understand me?"

Nobody says a word. Grandma Horace seals her lips

together in a quivery pink line, and Becksie whispers, "But how are you gonna pay for the doctor, Mama?"

Emmett speaks up with a mouthful of biscuit. "Yeah, how? Have the checks stopped floating yet? Or are they kiting this month? Which is it, Mama?"

Mama whirls around and grabs him by the yellow hair, her eyes on fire. "I'll snatch you bald-headed, boy, and don't you forget it. You know for someone who got to spend the entire day with his daddy yesterday, you sure are acting ugly this morning."

"Ow, my hair," Emmett cries. "I'm sorry. Sorry. Where is Daddy anyway?"

Mama lets his hair go, and Grandma Horace answers all stiff-like, "Your daddy will meet us later. As for the money to pay the doctor, it's mine. As long as Gentle goes to my eye doctor in Enka, I'll pay. Not that it's any of y'all children's business."

Mama takes off her apron and smoothes down her hair. "Your daddy left early this morning to play his banjo in the Buncombe County shoe commercial. One of his musician buddies picked him up. Now Livy Two, you get in there and wash up better. You look like you been kissing a cow's behind. Scrub those elbows too."

While I'm washing my face, Emmett comes over to the sink and whispers to me, "Guess what? I forgot to tell you, but I saw Ghost Town in the Sky yesterday,

Livy Two. Just the entrance. Look at it yourself when you drive past it today. Tell me what you think. And guess what else? I saw the newspaper in town yesterday, and I read that the astronauts are gonna launch a space ship toward Venus in a month or so. It's called the space probe *Mariner*."

"Venus?" I ask. "Why Venus?"

"Why not?" Emmett says. "I reckon if the United States is aiming for Venus, I ought to be able to aim for Ghost Town in the Sky." He scoops up Cyrus and Caroline and says, "Hey, let's go see the new, fancy pinecone palace of Uncle Hazard's."

I suddenly remember Emmett's plans to leave soon. Does he really mean it? I can't be sure. I ain't said nothing about it to nobody like I promised him, but I wish I could slow time down, make my brother content to stay with us a little longer.

A rocket ship to Venus . . .
a chairlift up to Ghost Town . . .
things is changing so fast. . . .
I sure wish they would slow down. . . .

CHAPTER TEN

Enka-Stinka

As we snake down and around the mountain roads, Gentle drowses on my lap in the backseat, a hot summer wind soothing our faces. When Grandma Horace takes the turns too wide, Mama makes funny noises in her throat from the front seat and knits faster. She's been knitting up a sight more lately: six finished sweaters, some pairs of mittens, and scarves and such, but she's put everything in the black trunk along with sweet-smelling sachets of lavender and mint that grow wild in the hills. She claims to be hatching a plan for all them knitted things but won't say what just yet, but I expect it has to do with money.

As Grandma hits the brakes to avoid a deer, she hunches over the wheel and says, "Car sounds worse than awful. I'm taking it to my mechanic. There's no telling what that musician of yours did to it."

"No telling," Mama repeats, looking out the window. We pass signs that say "Quilts for Sale" and "Get Granny's Apple Butter Here" and a funny one that says "The Wages of Sin Is Death. Quit before Pay Day." I have no idea what it means, but the words are posted on a sign in front of a little white church propped up on cinder blocks. I spot a seam of coal along the mountainside where some of the mining companies have set up strip mines, and it looks like teeth gashes in the side of the mountain. Some folks do work down in the mines not too far from here too, but Daddy says he could never be a coalminer and work down in the darkness, not knowing if it's day or night.

Along the road into town in Maggie Valley, I spy Miss Attickson standing on the steps of the lending library truck, and I wave to her like crazy, but she's too busy watering the flowers in the boxes hooked to the truck windows to see me. Then I see Mathew the Mennonite with his two little girls in sky blue bonnets, riding in the back of his painted black truck. They wave, and I wave back.

I lean over the front seat and say, "Can we invite Mathew the Mennonite's girls over to play sometime? Please? They seem awful nice, Mama. Wouldn't you like to get to know them?"

Mama turns around to face me. "Girl, you got a family full of children to play with, now hush."

"But I like to meet new folks too, Mama. They might become my best friends, and I don't even know it yet."

"Now Livy Two, you know those Mennonites keep to themselves. You'd do better to try and be sweeter to Becksie and Jitters. They're not so bad, you know."

"Ha!" I fix my eyes on the passing scenery. "I want me a wild best friend to eat mountain water taffy, make up songs about Maggie Valley, climb trees, and swing from vines with. I expect I'll have best friends someday, but not them two."

Mama don't answer. Instead, she closes her eyes and sings "In the Shadow of the Pines," another lonesome mountain song.

As we drive down Highway 19, sure enough, I spy Emmett's greatest secret longing on earth: Ghost Town in the Sky, big as Dallas, with a chairlift riding folks up and over the mountains. It truly is a kind of miracle, and I understand what my brother means.

"Look!" I yell. "That's the place where you can ride up and down the mountain in a chairlift." I shut up quick as I say it, though, so I don't let Emmett's secret escape my lips. A promise is a promise.

"Pure tomfoolery." Grandma Horace puts her foot

on the gas and more black smoke hacks out of the back. "Heavens, eight dollars to take a ride on a chairlift up a mountain to that tourist trap?"

"Kids ride free," I say. "Besides, I'd like to see what's on the other side."

"A money trap is on the other side, that's what, granddaughter."

"I want to see the money trap for myself."

Grandma Horace snorts, but Mama keeps quiet. I whisper in Gentle's ear, "Would you like to go up the chairlift to the Ghost Town in the Sky one day?" I pull her closer to me, and she curls her legs around me and whispers, "Ghost Town in the Sky."

At Dr. Johnson's office down in Enka, things get real quiet and serious. The doctor's fussy assistant makes me wait outside to study the *Life* magazine where all the ladies in the advertisements don't look nothing like the folks in this holler. The ladies wear lime green britches, pillbox hats, and tangerine dresses, and they all got swirls of hair that swoops up into what they call "bouffant styles." I'd feel a right fool getting all gussied up with sprays and perfumes in all that lime green. Heck, I wouldn't even know where to start. I do want to see the world, but I surely do wonder how and whether I'll fit into it. I study the pictures some more, trying to work out how those ladies can get their hair to stay put when all of a sudden, I hear a mess of screaming and shouting from inside the exam room. Gentle is kicking and screaming to beat the band. The assistant signals me to get in there quick. When I do, Grandma Horace is telling her to act right even if she can't see good, but Gentle ain't having any of it.

Mama pulls her aside and says, "Gentle, what do you want?"

"Livy Two!" comes the answer.

So now she's got me right by her side, and Grandma Horace stands way over by the window. Dr. Johnson smiles at me, and I like her right away. For one thing, she is a woman eye doctor, and I have never met an eye doctor before, much less a woman doctor. Neither has Grandma Horace, who asks, "Pardon me, but where is the real Dr. Johnson?"

"Do you mean my father? He retired, Mrs. Horace. I've taken over his practice."

Grandma Horace considers this for a moment before she says, "I hope you know what you're doing. Your daddy's one tough act to follow."

But Dr. Johnson turns to Gentle and says, "Gentle, my name is Dr. Adeline Johnson. But you can call me Dr. Addie." The doctor peers into Gentle's lilac eyes with this big old light that must see clear to the back of her head.

Gentle repeats, "Dr. Addie."

I like the way Dr. Johnson talks to Gentle, and my sister works her fingers over Dr. Johnson's face. Gentle doesn't usually do that with strangers. Dr. Johnson has strong hands that don't move fast, and when she talks, her words come out in a thoughtful voice as if she's been thinking about it for some time. She also has freckles and bright red hair that keeps trying to escape the bun at the back of her head.

Dr. Johnson writes something down on her chart. I try to see what she is writing, but Mama pats my leg for me to be still. Next, Dr. Johnson puts drops in Gentle's eyes. I can tell Mama is nervous since she takes out a bunch of yarn from her purse along with her knitting needles. I've decided that Mama knits when her nerves get to her, the same way Emmett whittles.

Dr. Johnson says, "That's a real pretty sweater, Mrs. Weems."

Mama nods, the red sweater with hints of blue and green on her lap.

"It might be for one of us, Dr. Johnson," I explain in a rush. "That's the way Mama does her knitting—she only decides who gets the sweater when she's done."

Dr. Johnson says, "Is that right?"

"Yes, it is," I say. "Mama is of the mind that a sweater has a certain personality and so does a kid. Money's tight, so it would just make sense if she sold a few, right, Mama? Daddy has trouble unloading baby food and encyclopedias and—"

"Is that a fact?" Dr. Johnson is smiling, but Mama and Grandma Horace stare at me horrified as I try to catch my breath. I am talking more than usual even for me. It's like I feel the snapdragons buzzing around in my belly, and I wish I could stick my head out the window and drink up the sunshine and fresh air.

Mama says, "My daughter can talk a blue streak with new folks."

Dr. Johnson says, "That's all right. What's your name?"

"Olivia Hyatt Weems. Livy Two for short. We already had a Livy One, my older sister, but she—" Mama gives me a look, and I know I'd better quit.

Dr. Johnson says, "It's nice to meet you, Livy Two."

I nod and bite my lips together. I like Dr. Johnson already, but I am afraid of what she is going to say. She squeezes more drops into Gentle's eyes, and I watch as Gentle's pupils grow real big and black. I squeeze her little hand tight, and she squeezes back. She sits real still, holding on to my hand. I wonder what Gentle does see? White clouds? Complete blackness? Gray?

Does she have pinpricks of light? She's never told me, and when I try to ask her, she won't answer. Her face gets a real secretive expression and she only cuddles to me closer.

Dr. Johnson leans down to Gentle and says, "Hey Gentle. Who gave you such a pretty name?"

Gentle ducks her head against my shoulder, so I answer for her. "Mama did. But my sister is shy, and I believe her eyes are a little sick cause she don't use them much. My sister Louise is teaching her colors, Dr. Johnson. And I aim to get me a book on guide dogs, cause we have this dog, a new dog, and it's my thinking that he could help Gentle get around the holler until her eyes get better. But I need to read up more on how to train him. His name is Uncle Hazard and—"

"Livy Two!" Mama warns. "Give the poor doctor some peace."

"You are a fine sister," Dr. Johnson says.

Then Dr. Johnson studies my sister's eyeballs some more without saying anything. I feel a tightness in my chest. How long is this going to take anyway? A clock on the wall grinds to three o'clock and stutters as the big hand hits the twelve and takes a deep breath. Daddy was supposed to arrive at 2:30. The walls are pale pink, with an eye chart on the opposite wall.

Finally, Dr. Johnson stands up and says to Mama,

"Mrs. Weems, I need to speak to you about what I'm seeing here. Would you like to have your daughters wait outside?"

Mama's voice comes out small. "I reckon my daughters can stay."

"Mrs. Weems, that is fine," Dr. Johnson replies, and suddenly, I wish we could stay suspended in the moment forever—the forever moment of knowing and not knowing, when there is still all the hope in the world that everything is fine.

Just then I hear some footsteps and doors slamming in the lobby of the doctor's office. I can tell Daddy has arrived, but Mama keeps knitting, almost mechanically—like one of them robots or something. It's like she can't stop knitting as she sets her gaze on Gentle and Dr. Johnson. Grandma Horace sits down next to Mama as Daddy busts into the room and yells, "Sorry I'm late. The session went over, but I got it! I got the commercial. Fifty dollars to sing and play on the radio about shoes. How about that? Not a callback, Jessie. I got it. Hear? How do you do, Doctor? Forgive me, one a them old boys gimme a ride in the back of his chicken truck. Hope I don't stink too bad, folks."

Gentle grins and reaches for the direction of his voice. He grabs her up close, and we wait to hear what Dr. Johnson has to say. Daddy gives me a wink, and it makes me feel safe. Dr. Johnson clears her throat and says, "There is a problem with Gentle's eyes as you folks suspected. Mrs. Weems, were you ever sick when you were pregnant with Gentle?"

Daddy jumps in with an answer. "I'll tell you, Doc, my wife got laid up with the measles bad, but I nursed her back to health. Good as new. All our children are—"

Grandma Horace interrupts, "Y'all never said a word about that. Not a word."

Mama says, "You weren't speaking to us then. A lot can happen in five years, Mama."

"You should have told me anyway." Grandma looks like she's about to cry.

Daddy continues, "Anyhow, my wife hardly ever gets sick, Doc. She's got too many kids to get sick. We need Mama healthy." His tone sounds like he's trying to shove happiness into the exam room.

"When exactly were you sick, Mrs. Weems?" Dr. Johnson asks.

"Right at the beginning when I was carrying Gentle." Mama nods. "The measles laid me low, but I got better, and later, the baby kicked up a storm inside my belly."

"Never a word." Grandma Horace dabs her eyes with a prissy handkerchief.

"I figured that was the case." Dr. Johnson nods but she looks sad too. "Mr. and Mrs. Weems, those measles affected Gentle's eyes. She's not able to see, I'm sorry to say. She's not going to be able to see as far as I can tell. It's due to something called 'rubella.' The German measles. They're dangerous to pregnant women."

I can't hardly breathe. I remember all of us covered with red spots and high fevers, but we got over it quick, except for Mama, who stayed in bed a week.

Gentle only smiles as the doctor speaks, and plays with Daddy's nose. She's too young to catch the full meaning of the words. Nobody breathes for a minute. Then Mama's knitting slips off her lap and clatters to the linoleum. She pulls Gentle from Daddy's arms and tries to find some words, but there are none.

I guess I knew Dr. Johnson was going to say something like that, but I was also hoping she'd say, "This is just a phase that Gentle will grow out of," or, "We have a miracle operation." I feel my shoulders ache, but I got to stand up strong for Mama.

Dr. Johnson says, "I've got some literature on blindness and the Braille alphabet. There's a school called the Governor Morehead School for the Blind over in Raleigh. I'm going to give you some phone numbers. A school may be the best—"

I interrupt her. "We don't have a phone, and Raleigh's far. Too far. Heck, I never even been there before." I am surprised at the brittle tone of my own voice. "So thank you, Doctor, but there is no way we're sending Gentle away to live at a school. She's not even three years old. And like I done told you, I aim to make Uncle Hazard into a professional guide dog to help her."

Dr. Johnson takes my hand. "I only meant for when she's older, Livy Two. It's too soon to think about now, but there have been studies that show that children who learn Braille early on are the ones who get educated, go to college, become professionals. You think about that for your sister. And most guide dogs are meant for older people, but I can't see any harm in training your Uncle Hazard to help Gentle find her way around."

"Livy Two." Gentle reaches for me, and I grab her from Mama.

"This girl is a fine sister to Gentle," Daddy says hoarsely. "She plays the guitar."

I see that Daddy is truly crying now, and Mama's got her hand clamped on his shoulder as if she needs the shoulder to keep her propped up. Grandma Horace's glass eye is staring right at Dr. Johnson, while her good eye seems to wander off alone, lost.

Dr. Johnson says, "I sure would like to hear you play someday. And Mr. and Mrs. Weems, I recommend a telephone. I'd like to be able to call you up to check on Gentle."

Daddy says, "Soon as I sell my——" but then he stops himself. He doesn't say it, and I'm relieved. Just like Emmett, I don't want to hear about the banjo hit today, but Mama says firmly, "I reckon a telephone is a real good investment. Thank you, Doctor." But then she shudders, and in that shudder, I feel a hollow pain that rises into the air, wall to wall, ceiling to ceiling.

I look at Mama, Daddy, and Grandma Horace, who look away from each other as if there is not a shred of hope in the world. But I have hope. Maybe I'll grow up to be a scientist and find a cure for Gentle's eyes. I could be a scientist *and* a songwriter, right? Marie Curie studied radium to help folks who were sick. The movie star Hedy Lamarr invented something scientific in radio waves that stopped the Germans from winning the war way back in the 1940s. So I can study eyeballs to help folks with sick eyes. But my stomach hurts. All I want to do is breathe in the mountain laurel that will tell me I'm home again.

CHAPTER ELEVEN

Howdy-Do Mae's

The white sunlight glitters on the sidewalk outside Dr. Johnson's office. We stand there not daring to peek at each other. A butterfly lands on my elbow and is gone in a flash. I want to chase it, cup it in my fingers, but I have to act grown-up and solemn-like.

Grandma Horace says, "Well, let's go out to eat. We've had a shock." I wonder how she can think of food, but I guess in Grandma Horace's mind, no matter how bad things get, folks still need to eat. Then I realize I could eat. I could eat a whole lot. Not to mention that I can count on one hand the number of restaurants that I been to in my life.

Grandma Horace steers us toward the car. "There's a diner up the road next to the gas station where I can get a new muffler. Get in the car, y'all. We'll figure it out."

Mama and Daddy don't argue but just stand holding hands real tight, dazed. Suddenly I can picture them, clear as day, at ages sixteen and seventeen when they were young and just meeting for the first time, hitching rides, skipping stones in Turkey Creek, having a Cades Cove honeymoon near Gatlinburg after eloping straight from Enka Courthouse. I set Gentle in the backseat and she arches up and demands, "Butterfly kiss. Butterfly kiss."

I lean down and kiss her cheek with my eyelashes, and she kisses me back with hers. Next, we drive to Grandma Horace's mechanic, Talkin' Harley Harrison, who stares at the car awhile, and cocks his head to the side in wonder after he turns over the engine and the clanking/rattling tune commences.

Finally, Talkin' Harley says, "I promise to get that muffler working so it won't act contrary on you no more." He has a bright silver tooth that glints when the sun hits it.

Grandma Horace says, "See that you do, and see that you do it quick. It's what I'm paying you for."

"Yes ma'am. I reckon so."

Then we head toward Howdy-Do Mae's Diner down the street. As soon as we set down together,

Jolene, the waitress, brings us frosty glasses of sweet iced tea. "Hotter than blazes out there today. How you'uns doing? Howdy, Mrs. Horace. Where you been keeping yourself these days? Haven't seen you in a spell."

"Fine, Jolene. Thank you. Right now, I'm on holiday in the mountains with my daughter, here. You've heard me talk about Jessie. This is Jessie's husband Tom, and these two here are my granddaughters." Grandma Horace says everything all hoity-toity, but I am impressed she knows the waitress by name.

"Nice to meet y'all." Then the waitress turns to Mama. "Jessie Horace? I think you went to school with my big sister, Mary-Ellen Nye." Mama looks at Jolene with that far-away look and says, "Did I?"

Grandma looks embarrassed and says, "My daughter's had a difficult time today. She's not herself. Would you bring us menus, Jolene?"

"Back in two shakes." Jolene waves with her long nails that curl like pretty pink seashells on the edges of her fingertips. Daddy catches me staring and gives my knee a squeeze under the table to quit it, but I'm too fascinated. Jolene marches to the cash register next to a dessert case that keeps twirling around in a lazy circle. She uses a spoon to scoop out change so as not to chip her perfect nails.

"How'd she get her nails to grow like that, Mama?" I ask.

Grandma Horace says, "They're fake is all. Put your napkin in your lap, child."

I never heard tell of fake fingernails in my life. Are they glued or stapled? How do they work? My eyes roam back to the twirling dessert case. Behind the windows are the most incredible sights: coconut creamy layer cake, cherry pie, lemon pie with mountains of meringue, swirls of chocolate pie, and big bowls of red Jell-O with castles of whipped cream. I've never seen so many desserts in one place in my entire life. I want to try me a taste of each one, and then I remember I'm supposed to feel tragic over my sister's eyes, and I'm ashamed to be hungry. Still, I whisper, "Gentle do you want a dessert? I bet Emmett wants one too. Let's take some home to everybody."

Mama says, "Sure, okay, darling," but her voice comes from deep inside her like she's in a sleepy fog.

Daddy ponders the menu as if it's one giant test. His eyes dart toward Grandma Horace who catches his worried face and says, "Never mind, I'm paying, Tom. It's worth it to me to see my daughter and grandchildren get fed. I been coming to Howdy-Do Mae's all my life. This used to be your mama's favorite place when she was a girl," she says to me. "We came here after she played Juliet in *Romeo and Juliet*."

Mama opens a package of salty crackers and feeds them to Gentle, not paying any mind to Grandma Horace, who seems to be gearing up for another spat. Gentle licks the salt off the crackers and nibbles the edges.

Grandma Horace plows on, "Your mama was also on the newspaper staff at her school, weren't you, Jessie? She designed the yearbook. My daughter was as smart as a whip. She had promise. So much promise. She could have married anyone, Tom Weems, you know. Anyone." Grandma's voice sounds shaky.

"Mama, that's enough." Mama puts her head on Daddy's shoulder. "Today is not anybody's fault."

"Married anyone!" Grandma Horace repeats. "Instead of running off to the courthouse in Enka, but stopping to call me from a pay phone first to say y'all were on your way to tie the knot."

Mama says, "We wanted to let you know—not just run off without a word."

Daddy adds, "How were we supposed to invite you? Who threatened to burn the courthouse down the minute we told you our plans?"

My ears perk up. I never heard nothing about Grandma Horace wanting to burn the courthouse down. I look at Mama, but she's miles away. It's like she's heard it all before and couldn't care less, but not Daddy, who looks fighting mad. He speaks in a strangled voice. "Who said, 'I'll burn the courthouse down, don't you do it! Don't you dare get married this way.'"

"I guess I had my reasons." Grandma sits up ramrod straight. "I could have at least asked the pastor to offer up a few words, but y'all had to have it your way."

Boyhowdy, this is exciting news from the past. How was Grandma Horace gonna burn it down? Use gasoline or maybe build a big old bonfire in the lobby? I want to ask, but I know better than to say anything or else they'll quit discussing it. Grown-ups always do that. Soon as you show interest in the subject, they'll up and talk about something else.

"Well, Mother Horace—" Daddy's face whitens— "I guess I sure am lucky your fine daughter chose to marry me, and don't think I don't know that for a second."

"Good!" snaps Grandma Horace.

But Daddy isn't finished. "How could I possibly forget it when you spent the first ten years of our married life reminding me how lucky I was to get your girl. Now ladies, if you'll excuse me, I guess I'm not so hungry after all. I had me a heap of roasted peanuts earlier." Daddy heads toward the door.

"Tom, don't leave," Mama pleads.

"Jessie, I just need to smoke a cigarette and collect my thoughts." Daddy heads out of the swinging door. I watch as he lights up a cigarette under the Howdy-Do Mae's Diner sign and gazes at the sky.

I feel a slow burning anger at my fingertips that rises all the way up to my neck and throat. "Grandma Horace, why do you got to talk so mean to Daddy?"

"Mean as a hornet," Gentle whispers.

"That's right. He's hurting," I say. "And you show him nothing but meanness, and I'm truly sorry to say that to you." I try to keep my voice from trembling, but it ain't easy. Angry as I am, Grandma Horace still scares the daylights out of me.

Grandma Horace pops her knuckles one by one without a word. Then she peers at me with her good eye and says quietly, "You're right. Sometimes I speak before I think, Olivia. As Mr. Shakespeare says, I need to mend my speech a little."

I can hardly believe she's admitting to being wrong. I look at her face covered with old lady face powder that has cracked in the summer heat, and, suddenly, I feel a little sorry for her. It must be tiring to a person having to be so right all the time about everything under the sun. After a short silence, I ask, "Were you really going to burn the courthouse down?"

Grandma Horace gives me a sharp look and says, "I

believe we'll all feel a whole lot better after we eat. And we'll get your daddy something to eat too. Don't you worry." She turns to Mama. "Jessie, what do you want?"

Gentle knocks over a glass of water. It's only a little glass of water, but it's enough to start Mama crying. She puts her head down on the table right there in the middle of Mae's and sobs like her heart is like to break. She whispers, "I knew. I knew." I pat her on the back, and Grandma Horace mops up the water and passes Mama a napkin. "That's enough, Jessie. Dry your eyes. This child has her health and spirit and a strong will. She'll do fine. There is nothing wrong with her brain, remember that."

Mama pulls herself together and kisses Gentle on the head. Gentle doesn't quite understand all the fuss. I can see that Mama knows Grandma Horace is right, but it's hard for her to switch from one way of thinking to another.

"Jessie," Grandma Horace continues, "are you hearing what I'm saying to you?"

Mama nods, and I think how funny it is to hear Grandma Horace call Mama "Jessie" and Daddy "Tom." I try to imagine Mama as a girl called Jessie coming into Howdy-Do Mae's Diner after a high school play.

Gentle puts her hands on the table and feels around

and finds the salt and pepper shakers. Mama tries to remove them, but Gentle holds on tight, stroking the smooth glass and metal tops. When Gentle pours the grainy bits into her hand and rubs them together, Grandma Horace says, "How do they feel, sugarpig? Do you feel the salt and pepper?"

Gentle just growls at her. A funny growl like Uncle Hazard when he chases after red birds in the holler. I have to laugh and so does Grandma Horace, but not Mama. She hasn't even taken a sip of her sweet tea. Jolene returns to take our orders.

"Ain't she a precious thing?" Jolene looks at Gentle. I can tell she doesn't know she's—I hate the word "blind," so I can't even think it yet, but I can tell Jolene thinks Gentle is normal. My sister's lilac-colored eyes are so clear that folks only think she's too busy thinking of other things. Mama says, "We'll have macaroni and cheese."

"You don't have to order the cheapest thing," Grandma Horace says. "Get yourself a hamburger or a steak and salad."

"The macaroni and cheese is for Gentle," Mama says. "She loves it."

"I'll take a hamburger, and a Coke, and I sure would like the biggest slice of coconut cream pie you got."

"Livy," Mama says, "there's no call to be so greedy."

"It's for Gentle too."

"Let the girl order what she wants, Jessie," Grandma insists.

Jolene nods with approval. "Coconut cream pie is our specialty."

As Jolene goes off with our orders, Daddy bursts back into the restaurant with a flyer in his hands. He shoves a paper in front of my face. "Hold up, folks. Livy Two, would you just read this? It says the Mountain Dance and Folk Music Festival is looking for new talent. The festival is coming up, and I want you to audition and play your guitar for the folks. It's a sight bigger than Settlers Days, I'll tell you that much. Heck, we'll audition together and play a duet. Me on the banjo, you on the guitar. Then you'll play solo, and so will I. How about that?"

"Tom, sit down, and order you up some lunch like the rest of us." Grandma Horace raps her fork on the table.

Daddy waves the paper like a flag. "Look, I know we had us some sad news today, real sad news, but this here flyer is good news. I could get some exposure with my banjo songs, and you, Livy Two, you could sing your songs about Gentle. Heck, you could sing all your songs. I know you got a mess of songs. Folks need to hear that beautiful voice you got, Magnolia Blossom

Baby. It does my heart good to hear you sing, and just think how you could make the other folks feel who long for sweet songs in their lives and don't even know it. We need to get our music out into the world, darling."

I shake my head. "I can't." I can't even imagine playing for strangers. I just play in the holler with Gentle and the other kids.

"But it's a genuine contest. We could even win some money."

"Don't be bothering this child about money." Grandma Horace sips her sweet tea.

Mama sighs, "We don't have to make any decisions right now, Tom. I can't hardly think straight."

But Daddy is on a roll. "Maybe it would bring in some money to buy some of those Braille books the doctor was talking about at her office. I can sign us both up today. What do you say, Livy Two?"

I don't know what to say. I think of singing in front of strangers and my mind goes blank. I've never even sung at Settlers Days and that's a lot smaller than the Mountain Dance and Folk Music Festival over in Asheville. "Would I have to wear a dress?"

"Heck no! Wear your overalls. It don't matter. Listen to me." Daddy grabs my hands. "When you sing with that pretty voice, you give me hope. Do you know how much folks need to hope? Do that for them, Livy Two. Sing your own songs and then sing one with me."

I look at the paper and wonder if I could stand up on a stage and sing in front of folks. I plain can't picture it, even if I had Daddy with me. I'm not like the Carter sisters or Loretta Lynn or Patsy Cline, who all sing so good. Those gals are not afraid to get up onstage, but they're grown-up women.

As if he can read my mind, Daddy says, "Look, you can try, Livy Two. You ain't gonna set there and tell me you don't have gumption to try, are you, girl?"

Mama says, "Leave the child alone. We've got enough on our plate today without making Livy Two a professional singer this split second."

"Amen to good sense. Singing in church is enough," Grandma Horace says.

"Oh Lord, not that again." Daddy signals to Jolene.

Jolene comes back to the table with her waitress pad. "Changed your mind, sir, and come back to us, I see. Well, what'll it be for you?"

"I'll have hamburger steak and French fries, much obliged, and some more of your delicious iced tea," Daddy says.

I look at the flyer which is all covered with pretty violins, fiddles, guitars, mandolins, and harmonicas. I think of how Emmett plays the harmonica so pure and clear when he lets it rip on a song like "Foggy Mountain Breakdown" or "Shackles and Chains." Maybe I could sing if I had Emmett with me. He plays all the real famous songs on his harmonica. I say, "I'll sing, Daddy. If you let Emmett play the harmonica with us on that stage, I'll think about it."

Daddy says, "Well, we'll just have to see if your brother likes the idea. If he does, maybe we can get us all entered. A brother-sister-daddy act. What they call a trio!"

"Livy Two sings," Gentle says. "Livy Two sings."

Mama says, "That's right, Gentle. Livy Two sings."

Pretty soon, Jolene brings our food on thick white plates. I put a spoonful of macaroni and cheese in Gentle's mouth, and she smiles. "Excuse me, Miss Jolene," I ask. "You don't happen to have Baked Alaska, do you?"

"No ma'am. That's one of them Yankee desserts, isn't it?" Jolene asks.

"I reckon so," I say, but add, "Then I'd like to order an entire apple pie to take home to my brothers and sisters. You can just box it up to go. Thank you."

Mama and Daddy both protest, but Grandma Horace says, "Let this child order her family a pie."

I eat the biggest hamburger I've ever seen in my life without stopping once. I chew on a piece of corn on the cob and a bowl of Jell-O with whipped cream and coconut cream pie. I want to cry it's so good, and I memorize every bite.

After we get done eating, Grandma Horace picks up the apple pie in a fine white box. She also pays the bill, which comes to a whopping $15.27, and she leaves a two-dollar tip for Jolene. She hands the pie box to me to carry, and I feel like I'm holding gold. Grandma Horace says, "Remember. That's for your brothers and sisters."

"Yes ma'am." I nod.

Then we go back to the auto body shop. Talkin' Harley grins at us, his nails thick with black grease.

"Say, whose bright idea was it to give the muffler some vitamin C and a coat hanger? That's the sixty-four-million-dollar question."

Daddy blushes. "I had to get home, sir. Didn't have no other choice but to rig up that orange juice can and make it a muffler."

Talkin' Harley says, "Next time you just bring it on in to me. All right, sir?"

"I'll be the driver of this car from now on," Grandma says, paying this bill too.

"Nobody arguing with that one, Mother Horace," Daddy says.

As Grandma Horace drives us out of Enka, Mama demands that we stop at the phone company on the outskirts of town. She marches inside with Grandma Horace, leaving us to wait in the car. Daddy drowses with his mouth open, but every time he falls asleep, he jerks himself back awake and shouts, "I'm awake! I'm awake."

Pretty soon, Mama and Grandma Horace come back outside with an order for a black standard telephone. Daddy looks at the order and says, "Why Jessie and Mother Horace, a telephone is just the thing."

Mama says, "A telephone man will come and install the phone in a few weeks. He'll bring it with him."

"The wonders of modern civilization," Daddy says.

"Not that you'd know much about it," Grandma Horace says as she starts the car, but Daddy just whistles and looks out the back window. She immediately drives over a few bumps in the road and orders me not to jiggle the pie. Pretty soon, Daddy and Gentle fall asleep. I am between them, and as we drive, I breathe in the smell of cinnamon baked apples. The car is real quiet as we drive through the valley, and pretty soon the aroma of hot baked apple pie is overwhelming, and it's right on my lap, warming my knees, and I figured, it can't hurt to eat one bite just to make sure it's good enough for my brothers and sisters. So I pull at the string on the box, which comes loose. Then I inch my fingers inside the box toward the crust. I dig out a bite and make sure I've got a chunk of apple. I put it in my mouth real fast, so I don't get caught. It melts in my mouth and is gone so fast, I figure another bite can't hurt. I dig out another and another like some lowdown pie fiend. The trip takes longer, as Highway 19 is crowded with cars lining up for Ghost Town in the Sky, and Settlers Days. I wonder if Daddy will still bring us down to Settlers Days, which goes on a week in Maggie Valley. Maybe he'll be too sad after today, but he chose the talent and Mama baked those cakes, so we really ought to go at least one day. With my mind a swirl of thoughts, I keep taking bite after bite, and before I know it, the pie is half gone. I'm horrified. Mama's gonna kill me. So is Grandma Horace. They'll both kill me for being so lowdown greedy, especially after I had that good restaurant meal. I'm a person who don't know the meaning of the word "quit." I'm so bad. Tears squeeze into my eyes. I got a sister who can't see and all I can do is gorge on pie. For shame, for shame.

Before we head up into the holler, I say, "There's the lending library truck. Let me out. I gotta see Miss Attickson about something real important. No fooling!"

For once Grandma Horace doesn't argue back. She stops the car, and I jump out and race toward the truck.

The day's been too much, so I do the only thing I can think of and rush into Miss Attickson's arms. She pats me on the back, but she don't ask questions, and I am grateful to her. I tell her I'm in a big fat hurry with the folks waiting, but what I need is a Seeing Eye dog book that teaches about training dogs. Sure enough, she finds me the book on guide dogs lickety-split. Miss Attickson never lets me down. As I go to check it out, she sniffs the air and says, "Olivia Weems, is that fresh-baked apple pie I smell?"

CHAPTER TWELVE

Twilight

After we get home from Enka in the late afternoon, Uncle Hazard and all the kids rush out to the car, except for Emmett, who is off fishing. Becksie and Jitters insist they did all the work and the kids are still alive, thank you very much. Becksie hands a wailing Appelonia to Mama, who has to start nursing the baby to hush up the frantic sobs. Daddy scoops up Caroline and Cyrus, while Grandma Horace holds Gentle's hand. Louise takes Gentle's other hand.

Becksie says, "What did the doctor say about Gentle?"

Jitters says, "Yeah, what'd he say? What'd he say?"

"She!" I correct Jitters. "Her name is Dr. Addie Johnson."

"A girl doctor?" Becksie sounds shocked to the bone.

"A girl doctor?" shrieks Jitters.

Cyrus yells, "How's Gentle?"

Caroline cartwheels and says, "Is there a weeping willow on your pillow? Hey, I rhymed."

"Inside now, children," Daddy says, and they all go into the house to hear the news. I don't go. I don't need to hear. I heard once. That's enough. I got work to do, but first I grab my overalls off the line and change back into them inside the smokehouse. It's a relief to be out of that church dress, and the denim feels good against my skin. I hang up the Enka-Stinka dress on the line so Becksie can't fuss at me.

Then I head out to the pinecone palace to study the pages of my book and learn that I could train Uncle Hazard from being a regular dog into what they call a "guide dog." It's different from a Seeing Eye dog. Them dogs are mainly for big cities. I want him to be able to guide Gentle around the holler and maybe through the town of Maggie Valley when she's older. First, I'll have to teach him to walk in a straight line without sniffing. Next, I'll have to train him to stop at the bottoms and tops of stairs, so he'll know how to warn Gentle too. I have my work cut out for me.

No time like the present, I think, as Uncle Hazard stares at me. I put a rope on him, and we march up and down the holler. I try to keep him walking a straight line without sniffing. The book says a dog has got to be able to lead a person around without stopping. Trouble is, Uncle Hazard inspects every stickweed and patch of thistle we come across. I say, "No, Uncle Hazard. Keep walking. No sniffing. Got that?"

Uncle Hazard rolls over on his back and wags his tail. He's not in the mood for a lesson, so I scratch his belly. "You're going to have to get serious." But he just wags his tail. I look toward the house where I hear nothing but an eerie quiet, and I know Daddy's told everyone. Soon, he comes outside with Gentle on the porch.

I say, "Did you tell them, Daddy?"

"Yes ma'am, I did."

Then Emmett appears up from the creek with three catfish hanging on a string, and I want to figure out the right words to tell him about Gentle, but he heads straight toward Daddy. "What did that doctor say, Daddy?"

Daddy puts his hand on Emmett's shoulder. "It's like we was afraid of, son. Gentle can't see. The doctor says—" but Emmett backs off like he's heard more than he can stand, and so Daddy quits talking. After a long silence, Emmett swings the fish around and says, "Say, look what I caught us for supper. Your favorite."

"How about that now?" Daddy barely glances at the fish.

Emmett says, "Hey, I'll put these fish up, and then we can play catch. Want to, Daddy? I found an old baseball on one of the trails near town. Let's throw the ball. I'll pretend I'm Roberto Clemente, and let's see . . . you be Mickey Mantle. How about it?"

"Not now, son."

"Come on. You never throw the baseball with me. Not ever. Just like you never taught me the banjo neither. And we hardly never go fishing. You're always on the road, gone, leaving me here with all these sisters and Mama, and now Grandma Horace. There are way too many females in my life. The least you can do is throw the ball with me, Daddy."

"Son, I said not now and I meant it," Daddy says in a low voice.

Daddy's mind is still way back in Enka in Dr. Johnson's office, but I can see Emmett's wanting Daddy's attention so as not to think about Gentle.

"Well, as usual, I can see you're too busy." Emmett shakes the fish at Daddy. They dangle like slimy puppets. "Or maybe you're too busy thinking about your banjo hit? How many more years you reckon it's gonna take you to write it? How many?"

"That's enough," Daddy says.

Emmett swings the fish in the air and declares, "How many, Daddy?"

"What do you want from me, boy?" Daddy sounds whipped.

Emmett says, "Why you could say, 'Them's the prettiest catfish I ever did see,' or 'Did you catch them all by yourself, boy?' or how about, 'Sure, I'll throw the ball with you, son.' Just about any of those things would have done, Daddy."

"Son," Daddy says, "I got a lot on my mind. Now clean up them fish for supper." Daddy goes back to rocking Gentle, but Emmett ain't about to quit so easy.

"Shoot fire," Emmett says, "I almost forgot to tell you. Why I killed a pack of wild bears today. Skinned 'em raw and cooked 'em over the fire. Then you know what I did, Daddy? I hitched a ride into Maggie Valley to see Ghost Town in the Sky, and I even filled out one of those applications, and they're a-gonna hire me to run the whole dadgummed place. They said they never seen such a boy with my talent who grew up on nothing but grits and fatback and turnips. They said I got talent a mile high and twice as long to boot. How about that? For the poor son of a baby food–selling banjo picker? And by the way, no letters came today from Music City, USA, either."

"That can be a good sign, Emmett," I can't help

yelling. "It means that the music men in Nashville are still thinking about it. Don't you know that?"

"Be quiet, Livy Two, I ain't done." Emmett turns back to Daddy. "Then you want to know what I did today? I got married. That's right. Though I'm only four-teen, Daddy, I got married, and she's the prettiest thing you ever did see. Mathew the Mennonite's oldest. Hell, I forget her name, but we're gonna have us a bunch of kids, like you and Mama, but I'm gonna make enough money first to feed 'em. Not like you, Daddy. I won't be letting my kids go hungry all the time like you."

Daddy sets Gentle down on the porch careful-like before he hauls off and hits Emmett across the face, not hard, but hard enough. I gasp, for as far as I can recall, Daddy has never hit any of us. Not ever. Emmett doesn't say a word as he touches the red mark on his cheek. He drops the fish in the dirt at Daddy's feet and takes off running.

Daddy yells, "You get on back here, boy! Emmett! Emmett! Son!"

I pick up the fish out of the dirt, but my heart is filled with a sorrow, deep and wide. As Daddy stares into the holler, I whisper, "You didn't have to hit him. Don't you know he's hiding how bad he feels about Gentle?"

Daddy's face tightens, but he keeps quiet. He covers

up Gentle with the quilt. I know he wishes he could have sold the banjo song by now—at least one of them. It ain't for lack of trying. Nobody works harder than my daddy, but sometimes folks just don't want to buy the poetry and songs that other folks make.

I go rinse the fish off in the spring before I take them into the house. When I set the clean fish on the table, Mama asks, "Emmett do that?"

"Yes, Mama." I don't mention Daddy hitting him.

"Tell him thank you. Grandma Horace is giving Cyrus and Caroline a bath. Say, Livy Two, did you get the pie out of the car? Your sisters sure could use a pie right now. Save some for Emmett too." I look at the mournful faces gathered at the kitchen table and bite my lip.

"Pie?" Louise asks, her eyes red.

"What pie?" Jitters and Becksie want to know, their faces pink with crying over Gentle.

I've put it out of my mind, but half of that Howdy-Do Mae's pie is still in the backseat of Grandma's car, looking mighty sorry and dug-at. What can I do?

"All right," I say, "but it's a rare pie. You got to eat it blindfolded."

Becksie and Jitters are suspicious. "What for?"

I fish around for an explanation. "That way you get to guess the taste and all the ingredients that went into the making of this very rare Enka pie."

They aren't convinced, but Louise saves the day and says, "Maybe it'll make us see like Gentle, eating the pie blindfolded."

God bless Louise. Becksie and Jitters can't hardly argue with that, so we go outside. Daddy and Gentle nap on the quilt, so I take my sisters around to the other side of the house. I set my sisters down on a fat tree stump. I blindfold them and feed them the pie, one bite at a time. "Gotta guess what's inside this fine Enka pie!"

"Apple," Jitters declares.

"And cinnamon," Becksie says.

"Good. That's right. And what else?" I say.

"That crust tastes like butter and lemon!" Louise says, giggling.

"Hurry up, keep eating!" I tell them. "You got a lot of ingredients left to name." I keep feeding bite after bite to my blindfolded sisters. Thank the Lord they can't see there is less than half a pie left. I make a vow to stop being so lowdown greedy. I also save a little piece for Emmett.

After they eat the pie, I tell them what Dr. Johnson said about Gentle. Louise says, "I remember them measles. Daddy took real good care of Mama."

Becksie nods, "He soothed her hot head with a wash rag."

Jitters adds, "He gave her broth and tea and played her songs on the banjo."

Louise whispers, "The way they looked at each other when Mama was so sick, it was like to give me the shiver shakes."

I don't say nothing. But Louise is right. Their eyes were so full of love that had no bottom. It felt like all of us children could swim in it.

In the early evening, I climb into the red maple to keep a lookout for Emmett. He's not back yet, and supper will be ready soon. Sweet corn, flapjacks, and hoppin' John, but I'm not a bit hungry after all the food I ate today. I breathe in the mountain air smelling so full of honeysuckle. It is twilight, and I whistle for Uncle Hazard, and he scrabbles out of the stick weeds and wild geranium patch with a cloud of a spiderweb clinging to his snout. I climb down the tree to help him. "Silly dog." I peel the spiderweb away.

Daddy wakes from his nap when Gentle plays with his ears. He picks her up and dances around the holler with her, singing about a Tennessee Waltz. Then he swings her, up high and says, "Smell the honeysuckle, Gentle? Breathe in the rosemary and those sweet apple trees. Feel it? This is your holler, Gentle. This is your home. Always will be, darling. Gentle's Holler, little girl. Gentle's Holler." Gentle spreads her arms out like wings as he glides her around the holler, sweeping her through the tickling leaves of the weeping willow tree.

Emmett doesn't come home for supper, so I head down the trail toward the creek where I spy him on a rock, skipping stones. I join him, and for a while, we don't say nothing. Then he says, "Did you look for Ghost Town in the Sky like I told you?"

"All I saw was the chairlift, but there was a line of cars a mile long into the parking lot. Is your face hurt where Daddy hit you?" I skip a stone five times.

"I hate him. Mr. Hit Banjo Man. Old Mr. One-of-These-Days!"

"He didn't mean it. We got awful bad news today."

"I know that, and I'm real sorry about it, but I can't change it. I can't do nothing about this family no more. I'm leaving first chance I git."

"You're not but fourteen years old, Emmett Weems."

"Daddy left home at fourteen."

"That was a different time. He always says so."

"I want to go out into the world and make some money. Get away from him."

"But I know a way we could make us some money," I say, taking the flyer out of my pocket. "Daddy showed it to me, and he said to ask you about it."

"He never asked me nothing about it."

"You never gave him the chance to, Emmett. This here's a flyer announcing the Mountain Dance and Folk Music Festival in Asheville. Daddy thinks we all ought to perform together. You and me and him. A trio. Banjo, guitar, harmonica. It's not until August, so we got time. A few weeks anyway. What do you say?"

Emmett looks disgusted. He doesn't want to believe me. He chews on a stalk of grass. Then he takes the knife and piece of wood out of his pocket and starts to whittle. I wish I could just make him be happy. Sometimes he's happy on his own, but it's like he expects others to make it all perfect, and then when they don't or it doesn't happen quick enough to suit him, it just gets him mad.

"We'd have to practice together. Will you at least consider it?" I ask.

"Maybe. But I ain't making promises. I tell you that right now."

"Fine."

"Fine."

There is nothing more to say, so Emmett and I take off our old shoes and stick our feet in the icy mountain water of the creek. The rushing water freezes my ankles and toes, but it feels so good after the hot sad day. Uncle Hazard bounds up the trail and flops down beside us. He puts his head on my lap and sighs. I lean back against my brother's shoulder, for suddenly I am bone-tired and want to sleep. Emmett lets me lean on him without complaint, and I watch the evening mist rise in the holler with my brother and my dog.

CHAPTER THIRTEEN
Settlers Days

A few days later Daddy announces that he's going to take all of us kids down to Maggie Valley in Grandma Horace's car for the last day of Settlers Days. Grandma Horace decides to let him borrow the car only because he's agreed to take all of us and give her and Mama some peace and quiet. Daddy says we need to recover a little from the shock with Gentle and what it all means. He also believes that it's only right that we go down and see what Settlers Days is all about in Maggie Valley. Daddy invites Mama and Grandma Horace to come along, but there's not any more room in the car. Besides, Mama and Grandma Horace want a day off from kids just to sit in the holler and not do a thing. I can't imagine either of them putting up their feet for nothing, but Daddy says both ladies deserve a rest. I can tell he's simply happy to get behind the wheel of the car again without the womenfolk telling him how to drive. Next to banjo picking, I think my daddy loves driving better than just about anything in the whole world.

We all crowd into the car, squeezing in the front and back seats, sitting on laps and whatnot. As we go to leave, Mama turns on the radio, and I hear the lonesome voice of Loretta Lynn filling up the holler with her new hit song called "Success," but I still love "I'm a Honky Tonk Girl," and I wonder what that really means—to be a honky tonk girl. Uncle Hazard bounds out to the car, itching to go with us, but Grandma Horace whistles for him to stay, and he bounds up onto the front porch to lap up some leftover scraps of hoppin' John from supper last night. We wave good-bye with promises to bring home a present or two. Daddy blows the horn, and Grandma Horace yells, "You drive safe now, Tom!" She scoops up Uncle Hazard in her arms, so he won't follow us.

"Yes ma'am!" Daddy nods as we drive down the winding gravel road out of the holler. It's hard to believe that we get Daddy all to ourselves for the entire day. It's almost like we can forget all our cares and worries for a few hours—Gentle's eyes, Emmett's fight with

Daddy. Emmett's going with us too, but he ain't saying much to Daddy. The two of them are keeping their distance, but everyone else is just happy to be going. When we arrive in town, Daddy walks through Maggie Valley like a king, with Gentle perched high on his shoulders. I believe my daddy is about the handsomest man in the Great Smoky Mountains, with his waves of black hair and big laugh. Gentle perks up her ears at all the fiddle players and cloggers come to show off their talents on the makeshift stages in the streets. Becksie and Jitters hold the hands of Cyrus and Caroline, while Emmett jogs on ahead to help with the pancake breakfast, but Louise sticks close to me, as she don't like crowds. We pass a square dance hall, and I hear the announcer calling over his microphone, "Grapevine twist, folks. Dip for the oyster, dive for the clam."

Since Daddy is one of the talent judges of Settlers Days, we get free tickets to near everything, including the pancake breakfast. This is a sight to see, because someone has hauled in a giant cement mixer, and the folks at Settlers Days have filled it to the brim with pancake batter. One of the volunteers explains how it will feed up to three thousand folks over the course of the week. That's a lot of pancakes is all I can think. Emmett gets a volunteer job serving up pancakes, thanks to Daddy, but what he really wants to do is hop on the chairlift up to Ghost Town in the Sky. Will today be the day? Since it costs eight dollars for folks over twelve, I think not.

Daddy takes us to see a blacksmith who fixes horseshoes, and later, I watch a serious game of horseshoes take place among the Maggie Valley men. Even some tourists get in on the act, tossing those shoes, hoping to win the grand prize of a granny quilt or some quarts of apple butter and blackberry jam. We stroll past the table of baked goods, and I see the last of Mama's cakes, one applesauce and one eight-layer coconut. One of the lady cake sellers, with springy reddish hair that looks like cotton candy, calls to Daddy, "Your wife's cakes were mighty popular, Mr. Weems."

Daddy says, "Thank you. I will deliver the message."

Next we come upon a stonecutter carving a limestone rock into the shape of a rose. His wife sits next to him, and she catches me looking at them. She says, "He used to make seventy-five cents an hour back in nineteen forty-seven over in Middle Tennessee."

"That sure isn't much money, lady," Daddy says.

"You ain't kidding, mister," says the wife.

The stonecutter smiles to himself, but keeps right

on carving the limestone. He's got a gnarled old face, and his wife says he's been carving that rock for days now, and how it's good a thing that it's limestone cause limestone will give easier than sandstone. I wonder what it's like to be a stonecutter, to dynamite rock out of the mountain. The old man says nothing but just keeps working that rock with his chisel and hammer. I can already make out some of the rose petals, and I wonder how he got the idea to shape a rose out of rock.

I pretend I am a stranger in these parts come to study the customs of the people. I discover that some of the ladies who make little apple dolls look like apple dolls themselves, with their wrinkled faces and gingham dresses and pinafores. I look for Mathew the Mennonite and his daughters, but they do not come to Settlers Days, and for some reason, this makes me sad. I want to meet them along the road somewhere and say, "Howdy! Come have a piece of pie or some cotton candy with us," or "Hey, let's go on up to the square dance hall and do the grapevine twist with the other folks."

A Cherokee Indian boy gives Becksie a free ride on the ponies, and I can tell she likes him because of the way her cheeks burn bright pink. Jitters don't like it one bit that a Cherokee Indian boy is paying attention to Becksie, and so she gets herself into such a lather that she falls off her pony. Good thing she don't have far to fall from the little pony, so it's more her pride that's hurt than anything. Daddy never lets Gentle or the twins out of his sight, and he waves to everyone in town. At the ice cream social we all eat whopping bowls of mountain blackberry ice cream. I don't want the day to end. I make up my mind to come to Settlers Days every year even when I'm an old, old lady and need a cane to walk through the streets of Maggie Valley.

Finally, we go to hear the musicians on the stage. Daddy gives me Gentle to hold, and she rocks in time to the music in my arms. I look around to see what Daddy thinks of the musicians picking onstage because he can be real critical of other musicians, but he ain't around. Where did he go? Then, as those boys finish their medley of songs, the MC comes out onstage and says, "Got a special surprise guest for y'all folks tonight. In the tradition of our Southern Highlanders, Mr. Tom Weems, a newcomer to Maggie Valley, will be singing and playing 'I Wish I Was a Mole in the Ground' on the banjo, joined by Ellie Ketteringly on the fiddle. Now Mr. Weems helped with the judging of talent all this week, and Ghost Town kindly spared one its finest workers, Ellie Ketteringly, so she could play you a tune or two. Come on out, Tom and Ellie! Ladies

and gentlemen, welcome these two fine musicians!"
And sure enough, Daddy and a lady come out onstage
and start in playing "I Wish I Was a Mole in the
Ground." I know it well cause I heard him play it
enough around the house—the same chords over and
over to get them right. I watch Daddy's fingers pluck
that banjo with pure joy, and the folks can't help but
start clapping. Ellie Ketteringly must be as old as
Grandma Horace, but her bow flies across the fiddle
strings like a bird in flight. The mountain music touches
the air, and I can feel folks just falling into its sweetness.
I love the way Daddy closes his eyes when he plays and
lets the music take him to far-off places. Then they start
in singing and playing another song called "The Death
of Queen Jane," about a lady dying in childbirth, calling
to her people to help her, and her folks come and com-
pare her to a rose in England. But as Daddy and Ellie
Ketteringly play, instead of thinking of Jane and her
hard birth, I imagine heaps of red roses growing in
England and wonder if I will ever see them on my ad-
ventures one day. Jane's folks are as sad as can be to lose
their red rose girl, but I can't help but see roses in my
head—fields and fields of red roses. I also believe that
if any of those music men from Nashville could see my
daddy right this minute, they'd sign him up in a heart-
beat. Ellie Ketteringly too!

As Settlers Days comes to a close, Daddy announces that it's still fairly early yet and we're going to take the long way home. This is fine with me. I love to go driving with Daddy, and I know he's feeling good since he played so well in his duet with Ellie Ketteringly. We hit the pavement going like lightning down the stretch of open road toward Asheville. Daddy's been driving fast ever since I can remember. He presses the gas pedal with all his might, and it feels like we're a flying pack of eagles. I wonder what Talkin' Harley would say if he could see Daddy now, or Grandma Horace for that matter. Soon we're going up to sixty, seventy, eighty miles an hour and climbing higher. Becksie's and Jitters's braids are flying in the wind, and the little ones grab hands and watch the dark trees rush by outside the car window. I hold Gentle on my lap, but I ain't scared cause I know Daddy would never do nothing to hurt us. His driving is as smooth as silk, and it almost feels like we're not even on the road, but gliding an inch or so above it.

He drives faster and faster, and pretty soon he yells, "Come on, kids, sit up and look . . . watch that old speedometer, now." Becksie and Jitters aren't watching a thing for they have closed their eyes and are singing an old gospel song about using a Bible for a road map, but me, Emmett, and Louise lean over the back of the front seat just as Daddy yells, "Ninety-eight, ninety-nine . . . hot damn, one hundred miles per hour!" Gentle squeals with joy, and we're all yelling, "Yay, Daddy! Yay!" He then slows down and chuckles to himself. He turns the car back around and drives at the speed limit toward Maggie Valley. We catch fireworks, exploding in streaks of color across the sky. Do they resemble the dancing lights of the aurora borealis?

Soon the twins and Gentle fall sound asleep, and even Becksie and Jitters begin to nod off. As the last of the fireworks rain across the sky, Daddy says, "Now, y'all don't need to be mentioning our evening joyride to either your fine mother or your good grandmother. That'll be our secret, children."

Emmett says, "Daddy, I sure wish you'd teach me how to drive."

"One of these days, son, one of these days. You're going to be a fine driver because you'll learn from the best, my boy." Daddy eases the car up the long gravel road into the holler where Mama and Grandma Horace sit waiting for us on the porch, but in my mind, my heart and head are still flying down the road at ninety-eight, ninety-nine, one hundred miles per hour!

CHAPTER FOURTEEN

Ghost Town in the Sky

A week goes by, and then Daddy gets word to audition again for Cas Walker's radio show. He says he's bound and determined to get it this time. With the fifty dollars already spent from the shoe commercial, he wants another job right away. A musician buddy picks him up at sunrise, and they take off for Knoxville, Tennessee. Mama says that a man from the phone company will be coming to install our new telephone in a few hours. She and Grandma Horace want some of us to go on down to the lending library truck so as not be underfoot, so the telephone man can install our new telephone in peace. Caroline and Cyrus will stay home, as they woke up with summer colds, but the rest of us will spend the day at the lending library.

This is fine with me, because I realize I need to check out some books in Braille, the reading alphabet of the blind and a teacher's guide, so I can learn it myself and start to teach Gentle. Uncle Hazard's a slow learner with the guide dog book, but we keep trying to follow the rules. He just has a curious nose and stubborn streak and don't like to wear a leash. Sometimes he gnaws on the rope with his teeth, whimpering and wanting to play.

Before we go to leave for the lending library truck, Mama nearly changes her mind about letting me take Gentle, but then she has to go to the bathroom all of a sudden, just as the phone man drives up to the house. He waits in his truck until Grandma says it's all right for him to come on inside. It's going to take him all day, since our house has never had a phone and wires have to be installed. Louise hides behind me because she's never seen a telephone man before and doesn't much like the look of him with his red, furry sideburns and baseball cap.

When Mama comes out of the bathroom, face all white and holding her stomach, that's how I figure out that another baby is on the way. Emmett also sees that Mama is feeling poorly, and I can tell he knows why too. Another kid. Us older ones are used to reading the signals of when a new baby is coming. Emmett looks none too happy about it either, but he keeps quiet as he picks up a stick and whittling knife. He won't meet my eye, and I watch as Mama sits down in one of the white rocking chairs and murmurs, "Y'all go on, but look out for each other good."

"Are you okay, Mama?" I ask.

"I'm fine," she insists, but she don't look it. Still, Mama's always sick at the beginning. I don't know how I feel about another baby. Seems like we have all the kids we need. But I guess another feels normal too, though I do not know where in the world we're going to put another kid. Appelonia ain't hardly big enough to leave the shirt drawer at three months of age, but at least her eyes are fine. I know because I did a check and took her outside the other day into the bright morning sunlight, and she blinked and squinted, and I felt such a huge relief.

As we go to leave, Becksie still needs to finish making the last of the black bean sandwiches for our picnic after the library. While I lace up Gentle's shoes, I hear Mama say to Grandma Horace, "We're just going to have to hire Mathew the Mennonite to come fix up the smokehouse. Make it into a bedroom. You could be happy for us, Mama. Take that sour look off your face."

Grandma says, "Happy? How am I supposed to be

happy for you? You're still nursing the last one, Jessie. You're not entirely uneducated as to how these things work."

"Mama, this is between me and Tom. He didn't have any brothers or sisters and neither did I. We wanted things to be different for our kids."

"Things are plenty different with all these kids running around. Enough is enough! Y'all don't have two nickels to rub together."

"I am pleading with you not to start in on me."

Grandma sighs. "Lord, I just hate to see you wear yourself out with—"

"You can go right back to Enka if you don't leave me be!"

Grandma Horace gets stone quiet and, after what seems an eternity, says, "Well, I am not going to pretend to be happy, but I guess it won't take too terribly long for Mathew the Mennonite to make the smokehouse into a bedroom to free y'all up some space in the house."

Emmett spits on the ground in disgust and walks off to go collect Uncle Hazard. I watch him put a rope on him to walk him down to the lending library.

"That is what I was thinking," Mama agrees. "Why, he could even leave the meat hooks hanging for the children's clothes, so—" She catches me listening close at the window. She says, "Livy Two, get going now. All of you!"

"Yes, Mama." I whistle for the other kids to hurry along.

No way to hear what Grandma Horace says next, as we leave the house and stumble through stick pods and rocks along the path toward the lending library. Soon we start in arguing over who gets to sleep in the smokehouse once it's ready. Only Emmett don't add his two cents. He walks way ahead, yanking on Uncle Hazard to heel. Louise, Becksie, and Jitters all tag along behind us on the mountain trail. Thank the Lord Cyrus and Caroline stayed home or we'd never get there.

Gentle reaches out her hand to touch the branches that reach out like fingers along the path. A crazy chorus of katydids screams like it's already night. I can tell it must be hot outside the mountains as beads of sweat gather on my forehead. It seems to take hours to get down the mountain, but it's only cause the heat has come on so strong. Jitters trips over a branch that snaps in two, and shouts, "It's too dang far to walk."

Emmett replies, "So go on back home, Mama's little baby."

Becksie answers, "Come on, Jitters, you can do it."

Jitters cries, "My knees hurt. My poor knees hurt."

Gentle yells, "Jitters's knees hurt."

Louise sighs. "Look at all this green. Let's pretend we're on safari in the wilds."

"How about we just act sensible and get to the library?" sniffs Becksie.

Louise says, "Then Livy Two, sing us a song that you're gonna sing at the festival. Practice for us."

"Don't feel like singing right now," I say, as I haul Gentle on my back. My mind is on checking out a stack of Braille books. I figure if I can learn Braille quick, then I can teach it to Gentle. With the guide dog books and the Braille books, we'll be able to help Gentle find her way in the world. I'm returning *Exotic Places* and *Huckleberry Finn*, and the e.e. cummings poetry book, but I intend to check out more books too. Books ease my mind from thinking all my nagging thoughts. I don't want to think about the Mountain Dance and Folk Music Festival that is drawing closer by the day. Daddy wants me to sing all my songs, but the judges only allow two. Daddy says I can sing bits of them if I do a medley, which is what he intends to do on the banjo. Then three of us will do a song together. Emmett and I have been practicing, though he won't say for sure if he's truly going to play or not. He only says, "Reckon I will unless something else comes up."

We wind around another corner, and sure enough, the lending library truck is just setting out there a-waiting for us. Emmett ties Uncle Hazard up outside and gets him a bowl of water. Then we all step inside the truck and call, "Hey, Miss Attickson."

I put my books on the return shelf, and Miss Attickson smiles at us from behind her desk, her short black hair tucked behind her ears. "Well, I was hoping I'd see y'all today, the venerable Weems tribe. I was lucky to get to make two trips to Maggie Valley in a week. That doesn't happen near enough as far as I'm concerned. Now listen, who needs apples? I have a fine sack of apples under this desk."

"Thank you, Miss Attickson," I say, just happy to hear her talk. She comes all the way from Memphis, Tennessee, and she speaks like a real lady. I reckon I could listen to Miss Attickson all the livelong day.

Miss Attickson continues, "Well, y'all children know what I say, don't you? Books and apples go together. One of my very favorite things in this world is to curl up with a good book and a crisp juicy apple on a lazy summer afternoon. You children make that a lifelong habit, and you will fill many a lonely hour. Books and apples. Small miracles, but miracles just the same." She speaks with her hands that flutter through the air like small birds. Then she is looking close at Gentle. "I don't believe I've met this Weems child. Who is the little one?"

"That's Gentle," Emmett explains. "She don't see so good, so Mama tends to keep her close to home mostly."

I let Emmett do the talking as I slip through the stacks to breathe in the books. I do so love the smell of fresh ink and clean, white pages with fine printed words. I run fingers over the bindings. Oh, I wish I could check out a hundred books for me, but I know I need to find some Braille books for Gentle. I glance at the tiny truck wall above Miss Attickson's desk where she has hung some of Louise's paintings—peacocks, a strawberry patch, and kids playing leapfrog in the holler. As I comb through the shelves seeking Braille books, Becksie explains, "That's right, Miss Attickson, this is our sister. Livy Two wants to get her some special books."

"Special books." Jitters nods.

Louise ducks her head down and keeps quiet, but I see she's got her eye on some famous artist book.

"How do you do, Gentle?" Miss Attickson says, taking my sister's hand. Gentle cocks her head in the direction of Miss Attickson's voice and draws closer to her.

When I have no luck finding Braille in the B's, I say, "Miss Attickson, I appreciate the guide dog book. It's a big help with training our dog, Uncle Hazard, but now

I need you to point me in the direction of the Braille books."

Miss Attickson wears a pair of red glasses, and her nose rises to a fine point. I can see I have stumped her with my question. "Well, let me think. . . . I'm not sure that—"

I say, "We need Braille books. The guide dog book is just a start. We got a lot of work to do, and I don't want to waste any time getting started."

"But I don't think we carry them, honey."

I bite my lip. I know it's silly to feel desperate, but I really want those books today. "But Miss Attickson, as you can see for yourself, we have us a sister who can't see good at all. We could use some real Braille books."

"That's right," Becksie chimes in. "Last year, our teacher taught us about how Helen Keller read Braille. Livy Two figures if we all learn Braille, we might could teach it to Gentle when she gets older."

"Teaching your sister Braille is an excellent idea, Livy Two," Miss Attickson agrees.

Louise nods at everything that's been said, her lips sealed. Miss Attickson looks at all of us pressing around her and then at Gentle, who stands there smiling. She kneels down before Gentle. "Sweetheart, I'm Miss Attickson. I don't have any of the books your sisters want, but I will bring them next time, understand?"

Gentle has no idea what Miss Attickson is talking about, but I do, so I ask, "Don't have 'em? Isn't this a library?" I know it might seem silly to some to get so worked up, but sometimes Miss Attickson comes to Maggie Valley and other times, she don't come for an age, and it could be another few months gone before I see her again. I feel like we don't have time to wait. Miss Attickson looks worried as she explains, "Livy Two, I'll order some special. I promise. Now I do have a book on Louis Braille, and you could read up on him."

But her answer ain't good enough. I don't know where my rage is coming from—maybe it's Emmett and Daddy, maybe it's Mama having another baby, or maybe it's my wicked, greedy ways, I do not know. Maybe it's everything all mixed up together, but Miss Attickson, who sure don't deserve it, is catching the storm boiling up inside my chest.

I try not to yell as I tell her, "We need real books for the blind. Today. Not stories about blind pioneers."

"Hush, Livy Two." Emmett grabs me by the elbow.

"You hush, Emmett Weems!" I shake him off.

Two little red spots appear on Miss Attickson's cheeks. "I promise that next time I'm in Maggie Valley, I'll bring some. That's the best I can do."

She can tell from the look on my face how much I think of that, but I don't want to make her bust out crying or nothing. But then Gentle picks up a book and feels the smooth pages with her fingers. Those pages don't mean anything to her. If she could read Braille, all the bumps on the page would rise up into pictures inside her head. Gentle needs pictures. The urgency boils up inside me again, but I try to talk in a voice that drips sweetness. "The thing is, we truly cannot wait a month."

For once, Becksie backs me up. "That's right."

"That's right," Jitters nods.

Even Louise stands there solemn, looking Miss Attickson in the eye.

Gentle smiles at the sound of our voices and says, "Books."

Miss Attickson leans forward and says, "You children are quite right. I'll tell you what. I'll be in Asheville on Monday. I'll go searching for all the Braille books I can find there and then I'll bring them on back here to Maggie Valley. And if I can't find any in Asheville, I'll go to Enka, and if I can't find any in Enka, I'll go to Waynesville, and if I can't find any in Waynesville, I'll go to Bryson City. I'll even head over to Tennessee to find some Braille books if I have to."

Already I feel a heap better. "Thank you, Miss Attickson."

"You're mighty welcome. Y'all are right to be so

concerned. And I'll even suggest that all the lending library trucks start carrying Braille books. It's the right thing to do, and I appreciate all you children bringing it to my attention."

Then Miss Attickson turns to Louise and says, "But I do have something for you, my dear." She reaches behind her desk and gives Louise five jars of thick tempera paint.

Louise's face turns red, but she whispers, "This is just what I wanted."

Miss Attickson says, "I've been watching you read that van Gogh book every time you come in here. Now you go home and paint another pretty picture for me to hang on this wall."

Louise shyly hands Miss Attickson the picture she painted of Gentle and Uncle Hazard and the butterflies, which Miss Attickson hangs on the wall with the others. Then Becksie gets down to business and says, "I want to check out this cookbook."

Miss Attickson says, "I bet you're a fine a cook."

"I am indeed." Becksie nods.

Jitters says, "I want a book on a mouse. I'd rather read about a mouse." Jitters knocks over a vase of flowers in her excitement, but Miss Attickson doesn't even yell as she mops up the water and puts the black-eyed Susans back in the vase.

Miss Attickson finds Jitters a book about a mouse, and then we all settle down to read, except for Emmett. He keeps looking out the window and pacing. He whispers to me, "We can't stay here all day. Let's go. Now."

I ignore him. I read the latest headlines from the newspapers that Miss Attickson puts in the periodical section of the truck. One says, "Marilyn Monroe Dead from Overdose in California." It shows a picture of a real pretty lady with light hair. I wonder what an overdose is anyway. Emmett keeps after me to leave, but I say, "We came a far piece to get here, and I ain't leaving yet. Go find yourself a car book or something."

I read books out loud to Gentle, who sits on my lap: *Make Way for Ducklings, Blueberries for Sal, The Story of Ferdinand, Goodnight Moon.* After hours of reading, Miss Attickson tells us it's time to go as she's got a long way to drive through the mountains. When we file back out into the sunshine to eat our black bean sandwiches, Emmett does it. He steps away from us and announces, "Now listen. I ain't going back with you. I'm going on to Ghost Town in the Sky this very minute, and if any of you'uns try and stop me, I'll let you have it. Understand? I don't care if you are a pack of sisters." He juts out his jaw as if daring us to cross him or stop him.

"Emmett, wait," I plead. "Stop. Not like this, please."

He pulls me aside and whispers, "Livy Two, I told you already that I meant it. I don't see no other way. Mama having another baby is the last straw."

"But I need you here, Emmett. Please." I try to keep my voice from shaking because I know how much Emmett hates girls crying and whining.

"I'm sorry, Livy Two. Bye now," he says, his voice high-pitched. "I'll write."

Nobody makes a move. I knew this was coming. We all know Emmett has got the itch to go. Daddy had it before him, and I reckon his daddy had it too. He reaches down to hug Gentle, but just nods at the rest of us. Then he turns on his heel and heads off in the direction of Ghost Town in the Sky.

"What about us performing together in Asheville at the contest?" I cry after him. "I can't do it without you. You know that, Emmett."

"I got other plans. That wasn't for me anyway. Daddy chose you." He keeps walking with his back turned on all of us. "He never chose me. Not unless I begged. I'm done begging."

"But I got it all figured out. We could split the prize money."

"I'm going where there are three meals a day and then some!"

He stops for a split second and waves at all of us

and then he is gone around the curve of sugar maples down toward Highway 19. Uncle Hazard barks after him, but Emmett keeps going without looking back.

"Traitor!" I scream. "You ain't nothing but a low-down traitor. I hate you, Emmett Weems, I hate you! You hear me, you lowdown skunk?"

My sisters gather round me as I cry. Becksie says, "Let him go, Livy Two. He'll be back." Louise and Jitters tug on me, and Gentle holds my hands.

We slowly start to make our way up the mountain path. There's a hollow spot in my heart. Becksie tries to make me eat part of her black bean sandwich, but I can't swallow a bite. I have no songs in my head either. What will Daddy say now that Emmett is gone? It feels like our legs are made of molasses. Even Uncle Hazard doesn't have his usual energy. He keeps look-ing down the path where Emmett left us, but it's like the woods just swallowed him up.

Jitters is soon crankier than ever. "My bones ache. Somebody carry me!" Just as I'm about to haul off and yank her braids, she stumbles off the trail and a low buzzing sound fills the air. I see two or three hor-nets zoom through the air from the woods, and my heart thuds hard in my chest as I realize Jitters has stepped directly into a hornets' nest. In seconds, the angry hornets fly up in a swarm and surround her in an angry black cloud. Before they can head our way,

Uncle Hazard spots those hornets and starts barking at them like crazy. He runs right into the thick of them, and so, instead of chasing Jitters, they start stinging him over and over again. I grab Jitters to get her away from the angry cloud of bees.

"Emmett!" I scream, even though I know he can't hear me. Uncle Hazard is now covered with hornets biting and stinging him, and I can hear his sobs of pain and rage. Becksie pulls Jitters to her, and I throw my sweater over Gentle. Then Louise steps forward and flings all her paints from Miss Attickson at the hornets. This seems to stun them, and for a moment, they look like flying bits of blue, green, red, and orange before they hit the ground. A thick rainbow puddle soaks our shoes as the hornets slowly drown in all the different colors of paint on the mountain path.

I'm afraid to move any closer to Uncle Hazard, who lies limp on the ground. He's all swollen up real bad with stingers and bites and welts. He's still breathing, but I wonder for how long. Mama says a mess of stings can be just as dangerous as a cottonmouth or rattle-snake bite. We can't lose Uncle Hazard and Emmett too. I hand Gentle to Louise and scoop up Uncle Hazard. I turn to Jitters. "Are you okay, honey? Did they get you?"

Jitters looks wide-eyed. "No, Livy Two. I'm sorry, I—"

"Good, now you stay with Becksie. Y'all follow me up the path, but I've got to run fast. Just follow the path."

Nobody stops me. They know I got to save our dog.

CHAPTER FIFTEEN

Oatmeal Baths

"**M**ama, Mama!" I tear into the holler carrying Uncle Hazard. Mama shoots out of the house onto the front porch with Grandma Horace trailing behind her.

"Where's Gentle?" she demands. "Tell me now! Where?"

"She's fine," I cry. "They're all coming right up the path behind me. But Uncle Hazard is hurt bad, real bad, Mama. See? Hornets got him. Hundreds."

I hold out his red, swollen body for her to see, and he's shivering from all those stingers, breathing funny. Every time I shift him in my arms, he lets out another yelp. Grandma Horace steps into action like I never seen before. "I'll get the oats. Livy Two, honey, bring the dog into the house lickety-split. We'll fix him up."

I follow Grandma Horace into the house without a word, and Mama pulls down the metal bathing pail and fills it with water from the kettle on the old stove. Grandma dumps several cups of oats in the bath and takes Uncle Hazard from me and places him in the soothing water. He doesn't even try to fight the bath, but lies limp in Grandma Horace's arms, his long ears spreading out like fans in the old washtub. I think of all those times he hated getting wet when it would rain or when Emmett would toss him in the creek to catch a catfish or just to have him swim. Now he floats in the water in Grandma Horace's arms, and she talks to him like he's a real baby.

"Get me some tweezers, Livy Two," Grandma Horace orders, and I run like the dickens to grab the tweezers that she keeps on the windowsill so she can pluck in the sunlight to see which eyebrow hairs need yanking more than others. I rush back with the tweezers, and by this time Jitters, Becksie, and Louise—bouncing Gentle on her shoulders—burst into the house. Caroline and Cyrus crowd together under the table, holding hands.

Caroline whispers, "I'll take his temperature. I'm a fairy too, and I can make him all better."

But Grandma Horace says, "Hush, not now."

Nobody takes their eyes off Grandma Horace while she bathes Uncle Hazard. Mama rocks Appelonia on her shoulder. Daddy's still way off in Knoxville for his Cas Walker banjo tryout, and then I remember Emmett is gone too, but I can't think about that right now. I help Grandma Horace hold Uncle Hazard as she tweezes the evil hornet stingers. Her wrinkled hands slow and steady, Grandma Horace pulls each stinger out and sets it on a cloth spread out beside her.

"Will he be all right?" Louise whispers the words I'm afraid to speak.

"Hard to say," Grandma Horace says. "Leave me room to see what I'm doing."

"Where's Emmett?" Mama asks suddenly.

Jitters and Becksie exchange looks. Louise sets Gentle under the kitchen table with Cyrus and Caroline. Mama studies Louise, who is covered in paint. "And what happened to you?"

Louise says, "Jitters stepped on a hornets' nest, Mama, and they swarmed around her. Uncle Hazard barked at 'em, and they started stinging him like crazy. I poured my paints that Miss Attickson give me all over the hornets, and they flew up in all these colors. Like flying rainbows."

"Then they hit the ground hard," Becksie says.

"Did you get hurt, Jitters?" Grandma Horace asks.

"No ma'am," Jitters's eyes get as wide as saucers. "Except for one sting, and I didn't cry. Not a bit." She sticks out her hand, which has a large angry welt on it. Becksie immediately plunks Jitters's hand in the washtub, and Grandma Horace tweezes out Jitters's stinger too. Although she tries to hold it in, it's too much for Jitters, and she starts in wailing. "Ow, owwww, owwwwwwww!"

"Where was Emmett when all this was going on?" Mama's got a one-track mind as she shouts over Jitters's sobs. "Answer me. Where is he now?"

"Gone up to Ghost Town in the Sky," says Becksie.

"Yep, Ghost Town," says Jitters, "to get himself a job."

"What?" Mama yells.

I feel a sob rise into my throat as I wonder where my brother is this very minute. On the road? On the chair-lift heading toward the place of his dreams?

Louise wipes the paint off her face and hands and says, "He was bound and determined. Not even Livy Two could talk him out of it."

Becksie says, "That's right. He run off before Jitters stepped on the hornets' nest and Uncle Hazard saved her. He run off just as we left the lending library truck."

Jitters quits crying and says, "Took off. Just like that. Gone."

Mama's face turns even whiter, and Grandma Horace says, "Now Jessie, you just sit tight. He'll be fine."

Mama says, "I'm going into town to make a—wait, I have a telephone now."

"I'll call Ghost Town in the Sky," says Grandma Horace, rubbing oats into Uncle Hazard's sores. "You take my car and go look for him, but you're not to worry over Emmett, Jessie. Your own husband left home around his age."

"My boy is not leaving home at the age of fourteen."

"No, of course not," Grandma Horace says. "He's just taking a little trip is all, and you go fetch him in my car and bring him on back home. Remember your boy has a fine head on his shoulders, Jessie. He's just like your daddy, Jessie, and he's got Tom's goodness too. Now take my car and fetch him back home."

Without another word, Mama hands Appelonia to Becksie. Then she grabs Grandma Horace's car keys and drives off down the holler to Ghost Town in the Sky.

I look at Uncle Hazard and ask Grandma Horace, "You ever seen worse?"

As she rubs Uncle Hazard with more oats, she says, "Why, in my day, you should have seen the hornets. Three times as big as these little hornet stingers." I know she's just saying those words to put my mind at ease. I see the scared look in her eyes. She's worried about Uncle Hazard too. Who knew that Grandma Horace could care about a dog? But clearly she does. Uncle Hazard looks up at me with sorrowful brown eyes as Grandma Horace tweezes out another stinger. A song slips into my head as I rub Uncle Hazard with oatmeal, hoping to take the sting away.

Uncle Hazard fought the hornets
like a knight from long ago.
Uncle Hazard sparred the hornets.
Now he's feeling mighty low.
Mighty low, mighty low,
Uncle Hazard's feeling mighty low.

"Thank you, Uncle Hazard." I lean down close to him. "Thank you for saving Jitters from the hornets."

I look out the window at the sweep of green pines dusting the skyline. I sure hope Mama doesn't drive too fast to find Emmett. I say a prayer to Livy One to keep an eye out for Mama as she winds down the mountain road.

CHAPTER SIXTEEN

Healing in the Holler

Hours later, Mama comes home from Ghost Town in the Sky without Emmett. She says she looked high and low but could not find him nowhere. When Daddy gets back and hears the story, he says we need to let Emmett alone for a while, and he will come on home when he's good and ready. Then Mama pulls him aside and whispers into his ear, and I can tell she's talking to him about the new baby, because he gets a big grin on his face and says, "That's wonderful. A new baby brings luck. And I got some good news too."

He turns to us and says, "Children, I got the job as backup banjo player on the Cas Walker show. How about that now?"

Everybody tries to sound excited and be happy for him, but it's like there's too many facts crowding inside our heads. . . . Uncle Hazard and the hornets, Emmett taking off to Ghost Town, another baby coming . . .

Becksie says, "Daddy, some letters came from you today from Nashville. Here they are. You gonna open them?"

Jitters says, "Yeah, are you? Open them up! Come on, Daddy."

Daddy rips open some official-looking letters, but it only turns out that the Nashville music men do not intend to buy the crop of new banjo tunes that Daddy has sent them. Daddy says, "Well, never mind. Cas Walker has seen the light to hire your daddy. That's our first bit of luck. The Nashville music men are next."

Mama doesn't say anything, but I can tell she is relieved about the radio show, because backup banjo player will mean some money. For now, we'll stay in Maggie Valley, but we might have to move to Knoxville if Daddy gets more work. Mama doesn't want to move to Knoxville, especially with another baby on the way. But I think she's more afraid that, if we left, Emmett might come back and not know how to find us.

~~~~~~~~~~~~~~

A few days later, Emmett sends us a letter with five dollars inside the envelope. Daddy reads the letter to us after supper one night.

> *Dear Mama and Daddy,*
> *Do not worry about me. I'm just fine. A-Okay.*
> *I got me a job at Ghost Town in the Sky like I said.*
> *Do not look to find me. By the way, I met your long lost uncle, Mama. Uncle Buddy. Grandma Horace's brother. He'd like to add a few lines to this letter hisself.*
>
> *Your Son,*
> *Emmett Weems*
>
> *P.S. Tell Livy Two good luck singing in Asheville.*

When Daddy is done reading the letter, he doesn't say anything. He just hands it to Mama and goes outside on the porch and picks up his banjo. He misses the enclosed note in the letter in Uncle Buddy's writing. Mama gasps when she reads it:

> *Dear Jessie,*
> *I would a knowed your boy anywhere. He's the*

spitting image of you. I'll look out for him. He's kin.

> *Yours Truly,*
> *Uncle Buddy*

P.S. How's my sister? I hope her glass eye doesn't give her too much trouble. I'm ashamed to say I was a wild kid with a slingshot. Give my sister my regards.

Mama and Grandma Horace must have read the letter about a hundred times. Mama writes him a letter back care of Ghost Town in the Sky with our new phone number.

It's strange to have a phone in the house, having never had one before. Sometimes we pick up the heavy old receiver just to hear the dial tone. Becksie and Jitters like to place bets as to who might be the first person to call us on a given day. They're also mighty sick of doing dishes and folding clothes, so they're taking regular breaks to practice dancing in the holler. Grandma Horace even helps them with something called the fox-trot. Louise is back to painting—using her raspberry and blackberry paints to make some new pictures. One's a hornets' nest with hornets and bees all the colors of the rainbow. I just keep practicing my songs on the guitar, trying to recall all the things Daddy said about hope coming out of my songs. I don't write to Emmett. Why should I? In my mind, he is still a low-down skunk of a two-bit traitor. I take a shortcut path down the mountain to look for the lending library truck, driving down Highway 19, but Miss Attickson ain't back yet with her Braille books.

Uncle Hazard ain't back to his old self. He lies in the granny crib most days, looking out the window as if he's waiting for Emmett too. Gentle sleeps with me now while Caroline and Cyrus sleep in Emmett's bed. Gentle hardly ever leaves Uncle Hazard's side either. She even curls up with him in the granny crib, and he licks her on the nose. This makes her laugh, and the two of them look like peas in a pod.

Grandma Horace gives him daily oat baths, and I help out. Then one morning as she gets on her knees to scrub Uncle Hazard, I say, "You been here a long time."

She gives me a look. "You worried that the witch of Enka-Stinka is going to park her broomstick here forever?"

My face burns red. "How do you—"

"Hush," Grandma laughs. "This place is pure boonies, but I like it, and more importantly, I like the folks in it, so Enka will just have to wait. All right with you?"

"It's fine with me." And it is. I feel like I'm getting to know a different side of my grandma Horace. I ask, "You reckon you might want to see your brother again?"

"I have no idea. He left a long time ago. Hard to believe he's back in the mountains again. He wasn't one for writing letters—a postcard every five years, maybe."

"What'd you two fight about anyway, when you was kids?"

Grandma Horace sighs. "How do you know we fought about anything?"

"Cause he shot your eye out with a slingshot one time, right?"

"The slingshot was an accident, Livy Two, and we were little."

"Why'd he leave and never come back then? What was it?"

Grandma Horace rubs more oats on Uncle Hazard. She looks at me with her good eye but doesn't answer. Then she says, "How about you pick out one of my glass eyes? What color should I wear today, do you think? I'm about tired of walnut brown."

My heart beats fast. Grandma has never let me choose a glass eyeball for her to wear, and I don't want to make a mistake. I peek inside her box that holds her collection. I study the different colors. Violet, blue, light brown, forest green. Then I say, "I think blue today."

Grandma Horace removes the blue eyeball from the box and says, "Well then, sparkling sapphire it is. Thank you, Livy Two." She pops out the brown walnut and puts it into the box. Then she slips the sparkling sapphire into her eye socket easy as you please. My grandma Horace is something else.

Daddy begins working regular on Cas Walker's radio show, and the talk continues of us moving over to Knoxville, since he can't depend on his musician buddies to pick him up all the time. There is also talk of buying a car if he can get some money saved. He gets home early one evening with a live chicken squawking in the backseat, which means Mr. Walker was throwing chickens off the roof of his grocery store today to stir up business. He says, "Well, guess who caught the chicken from the rooftop of Mr. Cas Walker's store? Bird practically flew into my arms. Looks like we'll have chicken and dumplings tonight."

"That's real good, Daddy," I tell him, but I do not intend to watch Mama or Grandma Horace chop off the chicken's head or see it run around headless for a few seconds. I seen it once in my life. That was enough.

I head off to the woods, but Daddy says, "Wait up, Magnolia Blossom. I need to talk to you." So we go for a walk together toward the creek, and pretty soon, he says, "Tomorrow's the day. You go onstage tomorrow night to sing at the Mountain Dance and Folk Music Festival."

"You think I don't know that? I just didn't think it would come so fast."

"Get that look off your face, gal. You're ready, Livy Two."

"Emmett was supposed to play the harmonica with me. How can I sing for the folks without him?" Even though I been practicing like Daddy told me, I still can't imagine standing up onstage in front of the folks. What do they want to hear from a kid like me for?

"You read his letter," Daddy says. "I miss him like the dickens, but if I go get him, he'll take off again. I love that boy, but he'll come on home when he's ready. Besides, Uncle Buddy is watching him. Who knew we had kin at Ghost Town?"

"Are you gonna be there when I sing, Daddy?"

"You think I'd miss my girl's big night? Now go on and practice that medley of songs you're going to sing."

"Do you like your job on Cas Walker's radio show?"

"Darling, you ought to see Mr. Walker. His show is on local television in Knoxville, and sometimes he struts around that stage while we're playing, carrying a sign that says, 'Fresh greens. Nineteen cents a mess.' He's a character, I tell you what. You know, Dolly Parton even started out as a ten-year-old on Mr. Walker's show, and she's already cut some records. A little old girl from Locust Ridge, Tennessee. Signed a deal with Mercury Records. Writes her own songs too, and she's just sixteen. I have a mind to take you with me to meet Mr. Cas Walker."

"Daddy, I'm happy singing in the holler. That's where I like to sing."

"Gotta branch out a bit, Magnolia Blossom. Folks need to hear that pretty voice."

"Daddy, I just wish those Nashville music men woulda bought your banjo songs you worked so hard on."

"One of these days, it'll happen. I will sell my banjo hit, and we'll all be sitting pretty for years to come."

"How can you be so sure?"

"Because once you sell one, you're in. Folks buy another and another. I just gotta sell one. You'll grow up and sell your own songs. You'll see." He hands me my guitar.

Then he says, "Almost forgot. That librarian honked at me from her big old truck and said to give these Braille books to you. I never seen one before myself. This is one here called *Braille Series 1960 Book Two*."

Daddy hands me a big book filled with raised dots. Braille. So this is what it feels like. I am so pleased Miss Attickson didn't forget. I run my fingers over the rows of tiny bumps on thick white pages. But how will I ever learn this secret language and teach it right to Gentle?

Then he gives me a picture book of Braille that goes along with Braille Series Book Two. It has actual pictures and diagrams of the Braille alphabet and numbers, which explain how it works. I look at the first page, which says that the letter *A* is one dot, *B* is two dots, one on top of the other, and *C* is two dots side by side. The dots are arranged in groups of six that are called Braille cells. And Braille numbers are like Braille letters only you put a number sign in front of a specific dot and that's how you tell it's a number.

Daddy also gives me two of my favorite picture books from Miss Attickson, *Horton Hears a Who* and *Crow Boy*, with actual Braille pages of the story stuck between each of the regular pages. Now I'll be able to read them to Gentle, but she'll be able to feel the dots with her fingertips, and I'll explain how they're meant just for her, and how someday, she'll learn to read these books herself and a whole lot more. Especially if we can get some money together by the time she's a little bigger, so she can go to over to Raleigh to attend the Governor Morehead School for the Blind like Dr. Johnson was talking about the day we found out the truth. I've been thinking lately that maybe Dr. Johnson was right after all about Gentle going to school and learning to read Braille. It wouldn't be for a long time off anyway.

Daddy says, "You think you can learn all that, Magnolia Blossom Baby?"

"I don't know, Daddy. Maybe."

"Tell you what. Let's just get through the Mountain Dance and Folk Music Festival tomorrow. Then you can get to studying on Braille for Gentle. I'll try learning a little too. We can all pitch in. One thing at a time."

"You think I can I do it?"

"I know you can, Livy Two."

Daddy seems so sure of himself and of me, so I set the Braille books down beside me and pick up my guitar, so I can practice my fingering, singing, and playing. He heads on back to the house to play with the kids, while I sing to the redbuds, the sugar maples, and the dogwoods. I sing to the wild geraniums, the pink lady's-slippers, and mountain laurel growing in our holler. I sing until I can't sing no more, and then I know I'm ready to face the folks in Asheville. I think of a new song for my sisters who love to dance, and I call the kids to come listen. I finish up singing to the tiny audience in the holler: Gentle, Cyrus, Caroline, Uncle Hazard, and who knows—maybe even some of the mountain fairies are watching from the treetops.

> *Jitters and Becksie danced the two-step.*
> *They cakewalked around the living room floor.*
> *They waltzed and they clogged.*
> *They dipped and they jogged.*
> *Jitters and Becksie, my dancing sisters.*

Then I play another song I thought of a while back about my brother and what he might be doing and thinking these days.

> *Go on and leave and see if I care.*
> *I won't miss you, I won't look for you at all.*
> *Go rambling, go wandering, go seeking, go drifting,*
> *but I won't look for you at all.*

CHAPTER SEVENTEEN

Mountain Dance and Folk Music Festival

Uncle Hazard barks up a storm and wakes me the next morning real early. I'm still full from last night's supper of chicken and dumplings, and though I feel sorry for the poor chicken from Cas Walker's roof, I'm glad not to feel hungry today. Mama will take the bones from the chicken and cook up a salty chicken broth and slice in some vegetables from the garden for more meals. Uncle Hazard jumps in my bed on the bottom bunk and licks my face. I take that as a good sign that he is on the mend. He leaps up on the other beds, giving everyone slurpy licks. He's back to his old self, and the only signs left of the hornets are scars on his shiny coat healed up to look like delicate pink kisses.

To celebrate, Mama makes biscuits in all different shapes. We have a little extra money from Mr. Cas Walker's radio show to buy more flour, buttermilk, and lard, which is all Mama needs to whip up a batch. We soak our biscuits in black strap molasses that Mathew the Mennonite's wife makes and sells in jars for a quarter. Daddy swears it will make us strong with iron. I guess we'll need it, because there is not a shred of dried meat left in the smokehouse, but Mama says that's okay because it's going to be an extra bedroom soon enough. Even with Emmett's bed empty, she thinks we ought to go ahead and get the smokehouse fixed up. Mathew the Mennonite plans to start working on it as soon as he can.

Emmett writes almost once a week, but he can't spell worth a lick, and his letters are too short—sometimes just one line. "I'm fine and the sun is shining brite," or "Worked at the Black Widow Ghost Mine helping Uncle Buddy, but I might get me a job at the Mad Hatter, the hat store in Ghost Town." I can tell Mama wants nothing more than to have her boy back home, but she suspects he's happy, so it's best to leave him alone for now. Sometimes Emmett sends money, and sometimes he don't. He says there are late-night card players at Ghost Town in the Sky, and when Grandma Horace reads that part of the letter, she sighs,

"Oh Lord." He also says that Uncle Buddy has a scaly iguana named Pearl that looks like a miniature dinosaur with its sharp claws and lizard eyes. I try to imagine my brother living with Uncle Buddy, a man near sixty who I do not know, and Pearl the iguana, and all those cardplayers with their late-night poker games. It's hard to picture it. Emmett's life is so far away and so different now. He's probably forgot all about playing his harmonica with me while I sing. Maybe he's forgot everything.

As it gets on toward late afternoon, I climb up into the red maple to get closer to the sky. I pray to Livy One to let the evening go okay. The sun burns through the trees, beginning its long dance toward China, and I know it will be night soon. My stomach turns somersaults every time I think of singing before all those folks tonight, but I hear Daddy saying I can do it.

Daddy doesn't get back home in time to pick me up, but he calls on the new telephone and says, "I'm in a hurry, Magnolia Blossom, so I can't talk long. Now, Livy Two, get Mama and Grandma Horace to drive you to Asheville, and I'll meet you there myself. I did more commercials for Cas Walker today and sang about squirrels and watermelon, which means I got money in my pocket. Things keep looking up."

"I'm glad, Daddy."

"And you tell your mama that I sold them two sweaters just like she asked me. You know there are rich folks in Knoxville who will spend ten dollars on a homemade mountain sweater?"

"They will? That's a lot."

"You bet it is. Be sure to tell the good news to your mama."

"I will, Daddy," I say, feeling like our money worries are just about over, what with Mama and Daddy working so hard together and finally getting somewhere.

Daddy says, "Now, I got something I need to do. Some business to attend to."

"Bye Daddy. I love you."

"I love you too." He hangs up first, and I give Mama the message, and she's right pleased about the sweaters. Next I take a bath and wash my hair in the creek with a cake of lavender soap, and I smell real good. I pull on a pair of fresh clean overalls from the line and Mama doesn't say a word about me wearing a dress. In the late afternoon, all of us kids and Uncle Hazard pile into Grandma Horace's car to head to the Mountain Dance and Folk Music Festival. Gentle starts in singing a song about a gal called "Jennie Jenkins," and we all join in with her. It helps to ease the cicadas buzzing in my stomach.

Backstage that night with my guitar, I look out over the crowds of people. The mountain wanderer, Mr. Bascom, sings a slew of songs he dug up from folks in the various hollers around Asheville and even invites some cloggers onstage with him. Harps, mandolins, fiddles, banjos, guitars, Dobros, washboards, and harmonicas serenade the warm blue night of August in Asheville. Mama sits in the audience holding Gentle and Appelonia. Cyrus and Caroline hold hands and sit between Mama and Grandma, and shout, "Yay for Livy Two! Yay for Livy Two!" Grandma Horace keeps an eye on Becksie, Jitters, and Louise, and Uncle Hazard pops his head out of Grandma Horace's bag and sits on her lap, wagging his tail in time to the music. My whole family is there wishing me luck— everyone except Daddy and Emmett.

Then, without warning, it's my turn. As a stage manager pushes me out onstage, my throat fills with a kind of terror I've never known before. I will never be able to get a single note out of my mouth. I open it to sing but nothing comes. I strum on the guitar, hoping that somehow the music will come to me. The audience shifts in their seats—waiting. I can hear shuffling, wondering, "Where's the music, little gal?"

My heart pounds in my ears and it feels like the ocean in my chest, although I have never seen the ocean, but I have read about the waves that crash upon the shore, and right now, all of them are heaving up and down inside my heart. How could my daddy make me do this and then not even bother to show up? He was supposed to sing with me. But suddenly, I feel like he's with me anyway, and so I take a breath and get started.

Sure enough, I find my voice, and I start to sing of Grandma's glass eye and how Gentle serenades the flowers that grow in Maggie Valley, of Emmett and Uncle Hazard fishing, of Becksie and Jitters dancing, of Louise's raspberry paintings, and of Mama's fiddle biscuits. I sing the songs of my family living in the holler. I sing for my sister Gentle, who smiles from Mama's lap, clapping her hands. I sing for Miss Attickson, who brings us stories and books, and I see her standing in the back smiling proud and happy. I sing for Mathew the Mennonite and his family even though I know they're at home, because as far as I know, Mennonites do not attend folk music festivals.

And I sing for Uncle Hazard—my brave warrior dog who fights hornets and plays with bears and who will one day help be my sister's eyes when he's strong enough to start learning again about being a guide dog. And maybe thinking of Uncle Hazard does it, but all of a sudden, I'm not scared no more, and I just let my voice carry me where it wants to go. When I'm done singing, I go offstage, but the folks keep clapping. A stage manager pushes me back out onstage to sing one more chorus of the medley. I do, and the folks clap some more. When I go backstage again, from out of nowhere, Emmett appears, gazing at the ground, his hands dug deep in his pockets. I can't hardly believe it. Before I can remember I'm still mad at the two-bit traitor runaway, I throw my arms around his neck, but he doesn't hug me back. He doesn't do anything.

I pull away to study his face closely. He looks funny—old, young, scared all at the same time. Then I see a policeman standing behind him waiting too. Emmett leans toward me and whispers, "Livy Two, it's Daddy."

CHAPTER EIGHTEEN

Daddy

I stand there with no sound in my mouth. Just two words. *It's Daddy.* I want to snatch back the moment before it continues, because, whatever's coming down the pike, I don't want it. As my brother tries not to cry in the corner, the policeman says, "Olivia Weems? We'd like to find your mother." But another policeman is already bringing Mama and Grandma Horace backstage with the kids. The next singer goes onstage and sings a song about drinking malted milk.

I try to listen to the policeman who talks low and urgent to Mama, but Grandma Horace shepherds us all away, so I only hear snatches of the conversation. "Borrowed a car to get here . . . one of his musician buddies lent it to him . . . driving real fast to make it on time . . . gravel in the road . . . strip mines . . . son waved down a police car on Highway 19."

"Where's Tom now?" Mama asks, her eyes downcast, but before I can hear anything else, a stage manager takes us back to the greenroom to wait. Grandma Horace's lips are moving like she's praying real hard. Becksie and Jitters hold the twins on their laps, and Gentle crowds in there too, all of them in a clump. Louise and Emmett look out the window into the night sky and wait. My mind is moving too fast to work out the details. Emmett was with Daddy? But before I can finish the thought, Emmett whispers, "Daddy came to fetch me at Ghost Town in the Sky so we could hear you sing."

"Is he dead?" I'd rather just hear the plain truth than try to guess what happened.

Emmett's lip trembles. "I don't know. They wouldn't tell me nothing. He's in the hospital. In Asheville. They took him off in an ambulance."

I still can't find words, so I say the only thing that will come out of my mouth, and it's so stupid. I pull my brother out into the hall, so the little ones won't hear. I say, "But he can't be dead, right? He ain't written that hit banjo song yet. He promised."

Emmett looks at me like I'm crazy, but I'm not crazy. I hear Becksie and Jitters sniffling, and Caroline and Cyrus start in crying. Should I be crying too? Maybe, but my eyes feel dry as the old cow bones we sometimes find deep in the holler. I whisper to Emmett, "You were there. You must have seen something. What happened?" Emmett shakes his head. He ain't saying nothing. I grip the neck of my guitar. My chest feels like it's bubbling with thick lava firecrackers, and I wonder why it's so hard to breathe. Daddy. Daddy.

In the days following, we move as if in a thick soup. Daddy was in a bad car wreck and has to have an operation to stop the bleeding in his brain, but they have to wait until it's safe to do the operation. Safe for what? I want to ask, but I'm too afraid. Emmett walked away without a scratch, and Grandma Horace says the angels must have been watching. I don't believe either the angels or Livy One were watching that good, or there wouldn't have been an accident in the first place. Mama sleeps at the hospital in Asheville, and Grandma Horace stays with us in Maggie Valley. Emmett's back home, for now, though I suspect he won't stay long. Now we really will need him to work and send money. Cas Walker's radio show folks send up a month's supply of groceries. Emmett remains tight-lipped about the accident, and Grandma Horace says I'm not to bother him about it, but I got to know.

While we move into this waiting game time, I keep waking up in the middle of every night, thinking I will hear Daddy plucking his banjo strings. The indigo sky hangs low over the weeping willows and red maples, and I call on Livy One to help Daddy be strong during the operation. Nobody touches his pan of peanuts on the porch, and before long the cast-iron skillet collects rust as the peanuts harden in the pan. Sometimes I believe I see him dancing with Gentle in the fields of sunflowers, violets, black-eyed Susans, and scrubs of Queen Anne's lace. I hear him tell her how this place is "Gentle's Holler," but now the holler feels different without him, like a chunk has been gouged out. Grandma Horace waits by the phone each day, and Mathew the Mennonite and his wife bring over beans and cornbread daily. We find it in baskets on our porch in the mornings. Mama comes home once in a while to change her clothes, but then goes straight back to Asheville to be with Daddy. Mama takes her knitting with her, so she'll have something to do while Daddy sleeps.

One night, I say to her, "What about the car Daddy wrecked?"

Mama says, "That's grown-up worries, Livy Two."

"But is the musician mad? Does he want us to buy him a new car?"

"No darling," Mama says. "He ain't mad. He says he's got other cars, and he says for Daddy to get better is all."

"But where is the car now?"

"Lord, you got to stop asking so many questions. You wear me out." Mama bites her lip and tries not to cry, but I need answers.

Grandma Horace comes in the room and says, "Child, get on to bed and give your mother some peace."

But then Emmett looks up from the corner where he's whittling something. He ain't said a word in the days since the accident, but he speaks real soft and quiet now. "I'll tell you where it is. The car is in the junkyard where they take other wrecked cars. That night, after he picked me up, Daddy drove fast. He loves driving fast, and you know it, Livy Two. Then he pulled over on Highway 19 and said, 'You want to drive, Emmett? Come on, son, you drive. Your turn now.' He said that since I've been itching to drive, now was as good a time as any to start. I told him I'd been practicing on Uncle Buddy's friend's truck in Ghost Town. He said, 'Well, then let's see you do it.' So I took the wheel and showed him, but I swear I wasn't driving that fast. Not nowhere near a hundred miles and hour. But I didn't see the rockslide ahead. I didn't see it."

"What are you saying, Emmett?" Mama's face has gone white.

"I'm saying I didn't see it, the pile of rocks, Mama, and right after it happened, Daddy was okay. He was okay at first. He had blood on his face from where his head hit, but he was talking right after the accident. Talking fine. He even made me switch places with him, so they'd all think he was the one driving, but right after we switched, he got dizzy and fell asleep. I kept trying to wake him up. I kept—" But Emmett's voice is shaking, and he can't talk no more. Not a one of us can speak.

Louise ain't painting no more. Jitters and Becksie ain't dancing or hanging clothes. Gentle sits on the swing and waits. The twins cry more easy now, and baby Appelonia clings to Grandma Horace like a fretful spider monkey. I want to play my guitar, but I feel like it's cursed, since Daddy was coming to hear me sing. I can't imagine what Emmett's going through in his head. Mama says I'm not to talk about it or blame him, but I can't help but play out every bit of timing and decisions in my mind. If not for that, then this. If not for having to stop, then that. I cry to Livy One and ask, Why? Why didn't she watch out for them? How can a split second change everything? More days go by in a blur, and Cyrus wants to know if the bleeding in Daddy's brain has stopped. Grandma Horace says, "Eat your cornbread and say your prayers. We'll know soon enough." Mama hardly ever leaves the hospital, and I miss her. I wish she would come home to sleep, but I know she's not about to leave his side. I want to talk to her about the secret sliver of hate in my heart for Emmett for Daddy's accident. I shouldn't blame him, but I can't help it.

After the operation, the bleeding quits, but Daddy slips into a coma, which is like a deep Sleeping Beauty sleep. Grandma Horace takes us to see him, but he doesn't seem to know we're there. We gather around the white hospital bed next to him and Mama, and I can see bits of his gray hair coming back. Boy, he wouldn't like that, and when I point this out to Mama, she says, "When he wakes up, I'll dye it black for him, same as usual."

I talk to him and all, but he just sleeps and sleeps. Can he hear a word? All of us talk to him except Emmett, who just holds his hand. Mama sits in a corner knitting a sweater. She's knitted two since the accident, her fingers flying with the needles. She says, "Livy Two, sing for Daddy. Sing a song for him." I try, but I can't sing right now. I tell her, "Next time. Next time, I'll sing for him." I write the song in my head, but my throat is too crowded with sadness to sing it. I only hum the song of Daddy and think the words in my head, but Daddy keeps right on sleeping his Sleeping Beauty sleep. A nurse comes in to take his blood pressure. I lift up Gentle and set her down by Daddy's neck. She reaches up and runs her little fingers along his face, but he keeps on breathing his deep, sleeping breaths.

CHAPTER NINETEEN

Getting By

The leaves change to burnt gold and red before they swirl to the ground. Uncle Hazard chases whistle pigs and squirrels, barking at them like crazy, warning them to steer clear of his holler. He also sits alert on the front porch, ears perked up, and I can tell he's looking for Daddy. I sit out there with him, scratching his belly. Gentle sits beside me, and I tell her how the branches on the trees will soon be naked against the sky, like bony witch fingers or lonesome spiderwebs. Gentle nods like she understands a little, and maybe she does. I've let her put her face against a spiderweb before so she could feel the silky threads on her face. I've also started Uncle Hazard on his guide dog lessons again, and he's learned to stop at the road, but that's about it.

After a few more days, Emmett goes back to Ghost Town in the Sky to live with Uncle Buddy. He and I ain't been talking much, so what do I care if he goes or not. It's a free country, I guess. Folks can do as they please. When Emmett leaves, he says, "Will you write me letters, Livy Two?" But I don't answer him. My heart is boiling with something hard that makes me feel ugly and lowdown cruel.

I know Mama's glad he has a job. Uncle Buddy is the night watchman at Ghost Town year-round, and he's letting Emmett work as his assistant, though pretty soon, Emmett might get to run the merry-go-round if he works hard. Uncle Buddy won't come down from Ghost Town to see Daddy in the hospital even though Grandma Horace wants him to visit. He tells her on the phone how he ain't never met Daddy in the first place and how much he hates hospitals and that he'll visit when Daddy's well again and not a minute before. He claims he doesn't want the first time they meet to be at a sickbed. Grandma Horace informs her brother that he has not changed a lick and hangs up the phone. I can tell she just wanted him to visit, so she could see him. It's been a long time.

A few days later, Uncle Buddy sends Grandma Horace a hundred dollars, and I see her breathe a sigh of relief. She counts the money and says, "Well, it ain't much, but praise the Lord for your great-uncle's good poker hand."

We start back to school in Maggie Valley, but I can't seem to concentrate, and nobody much talks to us anyway. I reckon they've all heard about Daddy's bleeding brain and deep sleep, and I think it scares them to ask. When I come home from school one day, there is a letter from the Mountain Dance and Folk Music Festival. I didn't win, but I did get an honorable mention and a check for twenty-five dollars. Grandma Horace says that's a lot for a girl my age. The folks at the festival want me to come back next year with new songs, but I doubt I'll have any.

One morning at breakfast, Cyrus and Caroline ask what "coma" means, and Becksie and Jitters just bust out crying and grab their prayer books like two little old church ladies. Me and Louise don't cry. It's like we know crying won't do no good. We just get our books and head down the path to school.

As the days fade into one another, the wind grows cold, and I smell the sharp bright chill of late September. Grandma Horace cans vegetables from the garden. There's more vegetables than we thought, even with the summer storms washing away the first two gardens. It sure seems a long time ago since Louise wore watermelon shoes and Gentle got lost in the holler.

~~~~~~~~~~~~~

All through this time, Mama keeps knitting sweaters by Daddy's bed and talking up a storm to him. She tells us on the phone, "Children, I don't guess I've ever talked so much in my life, and I'm not about to stop." She's already knitted up ten more sweaters. I don't know how she does it so fast, but she sits by Daddy, talking and knitting, knitting and talking. I know she's forming a plan in her mind, but I know better than to ask what.

Still, for all her talking, the doctors say that Daddy might not wake up for a long time, and we all have to get used to that, but Mama says, "To hell with that." The doctors explain to her that there's nothing much more that they can do for him, so a decision is made to move him to a home in Asheville with other Sleeping Beauty patients.

I ask Mama how we're going to afford this place. Mama says, "It's a county hospital. We don't have to pay. The state pays for your daddy's care. We can't do a private hospital. That would mean my mama selling her home, and we can't ask her to do such a thing."

When we go to visit him in this place, it feels very different from the hospital. It's darker and smells funny—like vinegar, ammonia, and rubbing alcohol trying to cover up other funny smells. There aren't so many nurses, but they wear spongy shoes that squeak on the linoleum like squirrels. Sometimes, the nurses come in and bend the legs of the patients or wash their faces, but not very much. There is only one doctor for a lot of patients, and he makes scratchy notes on paper that I try to read but can't.

I pretend it's not ugly and smelly in this sad hospital of Sleeping Beauty patients. I make sure Daddy's curtain by his bed is open, so he gets some warm sun on his sleeping face. His roommate has been asleep for ten years. Ten years! Some of the Sleeping Beauty patients have nobody to visit them. Then I stop calling them Sleeping Beauty patients because they look more like Rip Van Winkle with the wispy gray hair, pasty skin, and chain-rattling snores. Besides, in Sleeping Beauty, everyone else goes to sleep too, for one hundred years, but we're not asleep—we're wide-awake and waiting for Daddy to open his eyes and look at us.

Finally, on one Friday in October, Mama comes back to Maggie Valley to sleep and doesn't go back to the rest home the next day. Instead, she takes a long bath and gets all cleaned up. Grandma Horace does the same, and then we drive the sweaters to Maggie Valley to try to sell some of them. Becksie and Jitters stay home to babysit the little ones, but me and Louise get to go. We sell five sweaters, but what's more surprising is that we also sell six of Louise's paintings. Mama brought some of the paintings along just to see if they'd sell, and they did. I can't believe folks would spend twenty-five dollars on a painting. Louise sells some old paintings from before the accident, of the peahens and children dancing in the holler. She still isn't ready to paint anything new yet. Grandma Horace keeps the money, and says we're saving every penny. Mama and Grandma also are charging more for the sweaters. Fifteen dollars instead of ten dollars, and the tourists don't seem to mind the price hike at all.

The following Saturday, Mama and Grandma Horace take me and Louise with them over to Gatlinburg, Tennessee, where they sell ten more sweaters for a pretty penny to even richer tourists, who think it's real quaint to buy a homemade sweater from a mountain family. But to tell the truth, I hate every one of those rich tourists who don't seem to have a care in the world. I bet they don't have any Rip Van Winkle in their lives who used to be a daddy. As far as I'm concerned, those tourists laugh way too easy when they open their wallets and say things like, "Aren't y'all folks just so quaint?"

I want to ask the tourists what's quaint about selling sweaters and feeding eight kids and another one on the way? But I say nothing. The tourists are all so happy and distracted with their own children, whose pockets are stuffed with mountain taffy and chewing gum. I guess they don't reckon that things can ever go wrong.

Mama's belly is barely showing yet. She says the baby will come in the spring, and she's got a heap of sweaters to make before the child is born. After school most days, I collect the last of the vegetables from the garden and chop wood. Uncle Hazard watches me from his pine-cone palace as I work. He hates to be cold, so now he burrows down under his blankets with the winter chill coming on fast.

Mama says we're not to cry for Daddy. He'd get real mad if he thought we were sitting around crying, feeling sorry for ourselves. She swears he's sleeping so long to get his strength back. I try to read my books, but sometimes the words just blur together, and I fall into a long deep sleep where I try to find Daddy in my dreams, but I only ever see the back of his head.

When the snow comes, our holler is white and silent. Grandma Horace lets Uncle Hazard stay in the house, and he sits by the woodstove in a patch of winter sunlight that hits the wood floor. Gentle sits next to him making bead necklaces. Grandma Horace taught her how to string beads together, and she likes doing it. Appelonia plays on a blanket on the floor near Gentle, chirping her happy baby sounds. She has two teeth now and drools more than Uncle Hazard, if that's possible. Once in a while, some of the ladies that Daddy met at Settlers Days send up casseroles and cakes from the Baptist Church in Maggie Valley. They invite us to come to church any Sunday we want, and Grandma Horace accepts. Mama does not. She says she has sweaters to make, but Grandma Horace makes us go with her to church. She says it will do us good to get out of the house, so we go with her on Sundays. I like singing hymns with the organ but I don't listen to much else. It seems like winter lasts forever, and I can't recall the sound of my daddy's banjo. Once in a while, I try to play my guitar, but my fingers feel stiff like they don't belong.

Mostly, I just keep studying the Braille books during the long winter evenings. I have the alphabet memorized now, and I can read some words and short sentences with my fingers, but it's slow. It's so tempting to want to peek and see if I get it right. I know Gentle's really too little to start reading, but I let her play with the books and run her fingers over the pages to feel the Braille. She can say the alphabet backward and forward, though she doesn't know what it's for yet. I guess she likes it best when I tell stories to her and the twins. We're through most of the fairy tales now, and Caroline and Cyrus like to act them out with Gentle. It passes the time.

One day near spring, I visit the lending library while Uncle Hazard waits outside. Miss Attickson has ordered me another Braille book for Gentle. I don't say much to her. I only want to be by myself these days. I'm weary of folks saying, "We're praying for you." If Miss Attickson says it, I'll surely throw up, because by now I'm pretty sure Daddy is never going to wake up. As I leave the library with Uncle Hazard, we walk along the road into Maggie Valley and come across a pale green clapboard house perched on cinder blocks. I smell someone frying roasted peanuts inside, and it's more than I can bear. I creep up to the window to see if it's all a crazy mistake, but I don't see anyone, and then I hear an old voice yell, "Whatcha want, gal?"

I take off running, so they can't catch me. I miss my daddy so much it hurts like a wound carved deep and bitter inside my heart. I slip up a side street toward the river and climb down the rocks. I cry and scream for my daddy. No one can hear a thing with the rushing river screaming so loud in the Smokies. I cry for him to please-please-please wake up and come on back home. I pray to God and to Livy One together to reverse time, and I'll never ask for another thing as long as I live. I promise to forgive Emmett if Daddy wakes up. Up on the crest of the hill above the river, Uncle Hazard barks at me. When I quit my tears, I crawl up the bank and join my dog. The river washes past us icy bright and full of sunlight.

I feel someone standing behind me, and for a moment, I pray that it's all been a bad dream, and it's my daddy standing there, but when I turn, it's only Miss Attickson. She says, "You all right?" She stands there in white socks and sensible brown shoes that lace up. She's forgotten her red coat, and I can tell she's cold. It's funny to see her standing outside like any other person. I've really only ever seen her inside the lending library truck—except for the night of the concert, but that night is still a blur to me.

"I'm fine," I say, but I can't look at her.

"I am worried about you, Olivia."

"No need to be." I am embarrassed, and I wish she'd just go already.

"Not only that, you forgot the Braille book." She hands it to me. "You left it on the counter. And I have picked out some other books for your sisters and little brother. My, I do love picking out books for children. It's about my favorite thing in the world to watch a child fall in love with a book. Warms my heart. I picked a Willa Cather book for you. I've been wanting to give it to you ever since I heard you sing. Anyway, I thought the twins might like *The Story of Ferdinand*. What do you think?" She sits beside me on the bank above the rushing water, hugging her knees close to her just like a kid.

"Who's minding the books now?" I ask after a while.

"I closed up," she says. "I have something I need to discuss with you."

"Please do not tell me that you are praying for me."

Miss Attickson is quiet. "I promise I won't."

"Then what is it?" I chew on the edge of my thumb-nail.

"I have a proposition. I know it's only March, but summer's coming, and I need someone to help me get the books around the mountain. Someone who can learn to check out books to the kids, stack the shelves, and clean up around the truck."

I let this sink in for a moment. Then I say, "But you go all over tarnation."

"That's right. I do. I drive through Waynesville, Soco

Gap, Balsam, and Hazelwood and plenty of other places too. You could come with me this summer, and I'd pay you to be my assistant. A librarian in training, you might say."

"I don't think so. Where would I sleep?"

"There's an extra bed in the truck. It's called a Murphy bed, and you can pull it out of the wall at night, but most often I will drive you back home and drop you off in Maggie Valley."

"You know, my daddy is still in a coma over in Asheville. They say he might not wake up. I don't know what my Mama will say to me having a job."

"Why don't you ask her?"

"Why do you need an assistant now?" I pick the delicate yellow petals off a black-eyed Susan like the game. *He wakes up, he wakes up not, he wakes up, he wakes up not.*

"Because I'm of a mind to start a summer reading program for children in these mountains, and I need some help."

"So it would be like a real paying job?"

"Twenty-five dollars a month, plus all the books you can read."

I do some quick figuring in my head. Would twenty-five dollars a month be enough if Emmett keeps sending money from Ghost Town in the Sky? It just might, but Mama might not be able to let me go. I been hand-ling Emmett's chores, but Louise and Jitters could do those chores in the summer. Maybe Becksie could get a job too, this summer in town. Somehow, it eases my mind to be thinking of future plans. I ask, "What about the fall? Is this only for the summer?"

Ms. Attickson says, "More than likely. Though I have thought about trying to get a library open here in town all the time. Anyhow, you think about it. You know, Olivia, ever since you've sent me off looking for Braille books, I've learned a thing or two."

"Like what?"

"Like how they used to have to hang out pages of Braille to dry on a clothesline just like they were sheets or towels. And how it used to be that Braille was just on one side of a page, and that's why the books were so big, but a man named Mr. Robert Atkinson, who was blinded in a hunting accident, invented a very im-portant machine so that Braille could go on both sides of a piece of paper. He used special embossing plates, and it worked. That made the books smaller. He even started his own talking-book system. Stone blind and look at all he accomplished."

"I ain't learned it so well yet, Miss Attickson. Braille. I've had other things on my mind."

"You will, Livy Two. You will. Now I got to get

back to the truck."

A red bird lights down on a branch of magnolia blossoms. I call after Miss Attickson and say, "I don't have to think. I'll take the job. I'll take it."

Miss Attickson turns and gives me a big smile. "Well, that'll be fine, Olivia. That will be just fine."

CHAPTER TWENTY

Black Mountain

*M*ama agrees to the summer job, so I go down to the lending library truck regular to learn how to stack and shelve books whenever Miss Attickson is in town. Life seems to be falling into a kind of routine, but then, one day in late March, Mama gets us up early and tells us to get ready for a full day of visiting. "Today's an important day, and we've got two places to visit today," she explains. "First, we're going over to see Livy One's grave on Black Mountain, and then we're going to see your daddy."

"Why today?" Becksie wants to know.

"Yeah, why?" Jitters says.

"Because this new baby will be coming soon, and it's going to be hard for me to go visiting as much for a while. So first the graveyard to give flowers to Livy One, and then to your daddy, who needs to hear your voices whether he knows it or not. Now shake a leg, children."

The twins sing and dance, "We're going to the graveyard! We're going to the graveyard!"

"Hush up!" snaps Grandma Horace, plaiting Caroline's hair into two thick braids, while trying to get the cowlick in Cyrus's hair to settle down and behave itself.

"You think Daddy's woke up yet?" Louise hugs a new painting she wants to bring to him.

"Ha, fat chance!" I tell her, and I mutter under my breath, "Not old Rip Van Winkle." But I guess I say it too loud, for the next thing I hear is, "What did you say, Olivia Hyatt Weems?" and it's Mama talking, and she ain't fooling around.

"Nothing!" I tell her.

She gives me a hard look. "I've got my eye on you, gal. Right now, I am Mama and Daddy, and I've got my eye on you! Understand me?"

"Yes ma'am," I say, but then I am saved by the sound of Emmett and Uncle Buddy hiking into the holler down from Ghost Town in the Sky, calling, "Hey and howdy! Who's home?" Turns out, Mama must have planned this whole day ahead, because

Uncle Buddy and Emmett will be joining us too. They appear out of the woods from the path to Highway 19. I mean I guess it's Uncle Buddy, since I've never met him before, but he sure is a sight to see. He is shorter than Emmett—and a wiry little man who is also shiny bald. When Uncle Buddy sees Grandma Horace on the porch for the first time, he gives a loud whoop and hugs her and tries to swing her around. Grandma Horace says, "Good heavens, Buddy, my Buddy!" and hugs her brother back. "It's good to see you. Real good, brother."

Uncle Buddy takes one look at all us children hanging back on the front porch, a little afraid of him, and shouts, "Hey y'all kids, want to see a trick? Want to see how I get this durned old bridge of teeth to stay in my mouth?" We inch a little closer to watch him squirt Superglue on a row of fake teeth in his hand. Then he shoves them back in his mouth and clamps down. "Stay teeth! I'm a-warning you!" As he starts to laugh from his belly upward, Grandma Horace says, "Buddy, you haven't changed. Not a bit."

"How'd you lose your hair, Uncle Buddy?" Cyrus wants to know.

"Well, I'll tell you, kid. One day, the wind just come and blew it all away in a gust. Good-bye, hair! Cried my eyes out too."

"Really, Uncle Buddy?" Cyrus asks.

"No, fakely!" Uncle Buddy laughs like he's just told the best joke in the world.

When Emmett heads my way, I go off into the house. It hurts too much to see him. Part of me won't quit blaming him for Daddy and for running off in the first place like he did. Grandma Horace follows right behind me and says, "I know you're steering clear of your brother, but I'm here to tell you that nursing that grudge the way you are, Livy Two, is going to fill you with a meanness that will haunt you all your days."

"I don't hate him." I turn on the radio to hear a snatch of Reno and Smiley and the Tennessee Cut-Ups singing "Hen Scratchin' Stomp," but Grandma Horace clicks it off.

"Let me tell you something. I haven't seen my brother in some forty-odd years. And over what? Nothing. We grew up poor too, and he promised he'd take me with him to California, and when he didn't, I cut him off. I wouldn't read his letters. If I'd taken the time to listen, I'd have known he was trying to say he was sorry. That he wanted to send me money to come, but I was too damn mad and too damn proud."

"Well, I guess he lied then, didn't he?" I look out the window at Emmett pushing Gentle in the swing.

"You have to decide, child, if a lifetime of hating is

worth it. But I'm telling you, it's not. Nothing is worth a lifetime of being mad. Now, my brother is waiting for me."

Uncle Buddy don't talk about where he's been much or mention a word about exotic lands. When we ask about his life on the road, he says, "Ah, what do y'all want to hear about that for?" He says he lived in Needles, California, for a while, and when we ask what that's like, he thinks about it before he answers, "Hot." He likes to whittle dolls the way Emmett does. I keep thinking about Grandma Horace's words, but I don't know how to make up with Emmett.

We pile into Grandma Horace's Chevy and drive over to Mathew the Mennonite's farm. Mama says Mathew has agreed to let us borrow his truck, because we need to caravan since we won't all fit in Grandma Horace's Chevy. When we pick up the truck from Mathew the Mennonite at his home, he says, "You'uns drive safe now." Mama says, "I appreciate this, Mathew." Mathew nods, and his wife comes out of the house in a sky blue dress and bonnet and gives us a basket of corn muffins and biscuits and a jug of lemonade to take as snacks. Their daughters wave at me from the window. The one with long brown hair under her bonnet comes out to the truck and says, "I'm Ruth. My daddy talks about you. Nice to meet you. My daddy says you play the guitar real good."

"I don't play no more."

"Why not? Maybe you should. Maybe you could teach me. I'd like to learn." Then Ruth smiles at me the way a friend might, and I can't say no to her, so I say, "Maybe."

Then Mama calls, "Young'uns, get settled back there. We got to get going."

I wave good-bye to Ruth and climb up into the back of the truck with Gentle. On the way to Black Mountain, we caravan with Grandma Horace and Uncle Buddy driving Becksie, Jitters, and the twins to the cemetery in Grandma Horace's car. Appelonia rides in the front of Mr. Mathew's black truck with Mama driving. Me, Gentle, Louise, and Emmett ride in the flatbed of Mr. Mathew's truck. Mama's got a stack of sweaters to give to a store in Asheville. She's been getting orders, so she just keeps making more. It's still not enough money, but I hate thinking about money all the time. Gentle is now beginning to learn the Braille alphabet from Miss Attickson's books. Grandma Horace began teaching her the day Gentle turned three. Now they sit down together, and Grandma Horace takes Gentle's finger and puts it on the *A* bump and says, "A." Gentle repeats. Then *B,* and then *C* and so on until they go through the entire alphabet, but I suspect that one day we're gonna have to find Gentle a real teacher.

Louise has also finally started painting again. The first picture she painted was of Gentle and Grandma Horace, but she only painted their hands, so you see this old, gnarled pair of hands with these plump baby hands resting on the pages of a Braille book. Now Louise is painting a picture of Caroline in her fairy wings flying over the mountains of Maggie Valley. Whenever Caroline looks at the painting, she says to Louise, "Make me even more beautiful. The most beautiful mountain fairy in the world." Louise ignores her and keeps right on painting.

As we get closer to Black Mountain, everyone's real quiet. I have to wonder myself if Livy One knows we're all coming to see her. Do ghosts hover above their graves? Do I even believe in ghosts? I always feel like Livy One is with us anyway, but I'm pleased to go see her grave. It's been a dream of mine ever since I was a kid. Mama was always too sad to come before, but now she's ready. I wish Daddy was with us. I wish he'd pop up along the road somewhere awake and strong again.

Hey, fooled you, didn't I? Come give your daddy a hug, you passel of fine-looking children.

Uncle Hazard climbs up on his haunches, and his ears fly back as Mama presses the gas on Mathew the Mennonite's painted black truck, but she ain't likely to be driving no hundred miles per hour. Me, Gentle, Louise, and Emmett bounce around in the back of the flatbed, and Emmett stares at the passing road signs. I like the way the sun bounces off his wheat-colored hair. I yell into the wind, "I'm sorry, Emmett."

"What?" he yells back.

"I'm sorry!" I try again. "It wasn't your fault. I know it was an accident."

"What?" Emmett shakes his head.

"She said she's sorry! Livy Two is sorry!" Gentle shouts at him just as Mama slows down to let another truck pass.

He hears it this time. He nods and says, "Me too, Livy. Me too."

As we drive through the Smokies toward Black Mountain, I think of how these mountains are older than the Rockies, the Andes, the Alps. I feel lucky to breathe in the sun and wind in the back of the pickup with my sisters and brother. I hold Gentle's hand, and she climbs up on my lap, smelling like warm apples and the fresh air of the Smoky Mountains.

When Mama pulls up to the cemetery gates, we all slowly pile out of Mathew the Mennonite's truck. There is a sign outside the cemetery and church that reads: "A short memory is not a clear conscience." I've noticed little churches always have those sayings. Grandma Horace calls them "thinking pick-me-ups" for churchgoing folks and sinners alike. I do not have a short memory myself. Sometimes, I wish I did, as all my memories pack themselves into my heart and head, and I long to blow them all away like dandelion puffs into the wind.

Uncle Hazard bounds down the path of the cemetery happy as a clam. I reckon dogs don't see no difference in a graveyard or a mountain holler. Caroline and Cyrus hold hands and follow Mama, who carries Appelonia. I hold Gentle's hand as I walk with Louise down the winding path toward Livy One's grave. I try to keep my breath steady and even. We let Mama go ahead first. It's her child. Mama kneels down and places a spray of bird's-foot violets and trillium on the grave. She caresses the headstone the way I've seen her touch the heads of the new babies who come to sleep in the shirt drawer and grow up into my sisters and brothers. She looks back at all of us waiting, and she smiles, and calls, "You'uns come on over here and sit down." I realize it's going to be okay. Mama's not going to cry today. She'll hold on until later, because right now she just wants to be with Livy One. We gather around Mama. The headstone says:

> *Olivia Hyatt Weems*
> *March 27, 1950*
> *March 27, 1950*
>
> *"I just wear my wings"*
> *—Emily Dickinson*

I realize that today is March 27. That's why Mama picked today. An ancient oak tree shades the grave in sweetness. Not far away, I can hear the sound of a brook running down the mountain. I look for Emmett, who stands by Mathew the Mennonite's truck. He folds his arms by his chest and checks his watch but doesn't move any closer. Then Cyrus runs back to Emmett— the two brothers among so many sisters. Becksie and Jitters take out the basket of corn muffins and biscuits from Mathew the Mennonite's wife. Mama pours the cold lemonade from the jug into cups. Louise takes out a pad of paper and starts to sketch the weeping willow. Uncle Buddy helps Grandma Horace sit in one of the folding chairs he bought, and the two of them sit side by side, looking like wizened apple dolls. Uncle Buddy whispers something to Grandma Horace that makes her laugh. It's funny to see a such an old, old brother and sister getting tickled like that together. The twins take Gentle's hands, and they skip together through the graves. I don't have my guitar, but for some reason, I feel like singing the song that's been rattling around in my head.

How do you do, Olivia Hyatt Weems?
How do you do, my sister?
You angel in cobalt skies . . .
You bird in crimson clouds . . .
How do you do, my sweet mountain sister?

Emmett takes out his harmonica and begins to play along with me. Mama adds her church lady singing voice that sounds so funny, but it feels so good to hear her sing. It feels good to use my voice again too. It's been a long time. Grandma Horace smiles at Mama and nods at her to keep on singing. Mama blushes but sings out clean and strong. Uncle Hazard thumps his tail and listens, adding a plaintive howl now and then to show his appreciation. Soon the other kids join in too. Then Gentle stands and sings the refrain of "How do you do, my sister, how do you, my sister" with a voice as rich and pure as mountain honey. Who knew Gentle had a voice that would surely make the angels dance? I fall into that voice that lifts us up over the graveyard, winding up through branches of the weeping willow, carrying us all way up yonder to where the first Olivia listens to the voices of a family on earth who will always love her.

I whisper a silent prayer to her: "Livy One, hold Daddy's hand while he's sleeping, and please tell him how much we love him. Please tell him that for me. Tell him I won't ever forget. Not ever."

When we pile back into the car to go to the Rip Van Winkle home over in Asheville, I decide I won't be afraid to see Daddy today. I'll tell him all about Olivia's grave. I'll tell him about e.e. cummings and Emily Dickinson and even about *The Song of the Lark*, the book Miss Attickson gave me about a girl singer from the prairie a long time ago named Thea Kronborg. He'd like that, I bet. We arrive at the rest home in no time flat. "Is Daddy gonna die like Livy One?" asks Caroline.

"Hush." Becksie thumps her on the shoulder.

"That's right, hush!" Jitters says.

"Ouch!" Caroline rubs her shoulder.

"I told y'all a thousand times, this one is not going to kill him." Mama combs our hair and straightens our clothes as we pile out of the car and truck. Uncle Buddy and Grandma Horace decide to wait in the car with Uncle Hazard, who is not allowed in the rest home. Grandma Horace says, "We'll be fine here. Tom needs his children today."

"That's right," says Uncle Buddy. "I got to finish telling your grandmother the grand adventure of my life."

I say, "Uncle Buddy, I plan to travel like you one day. Did you have an itch in your bones to visit exotic lands too? Like swim in the Ganges River or lay your eyes on the aurora borealis?"

Uncle Buddy looks at me, confused, and says, "Speak English, kid." He busts out laughing, holding his sides. I don't see what's so funny, but Emmett leans over and says, "You just got to get used to him is all."

Mama says, "Never mind. Come on, plenty of time for questions later." She prods us toward the front door of the Rip Van Winkle rest home, and soon we're inside, walking along the halls, the odor of disinfectant, vinegar, rubbing alcohol, and other unknown smells filling our noses. We enter Daddy's room and crowd around his bed. He has three other Rip Van

Winkle roommates now. Mama holds Appelonia on her hip and says, "Now, I want each of you to say something to him. Talk to him normal like he was coming home from a day at Cas Walker's radio show."

Becksie goes first and says, "I been praying for you, Daddy. And I might get a job in town this summer. I was thinking a mountain café would be real nice. What do you think?"

Jitters echoes, "Me too. I have several job interviews, but nothing yet."

Louise says, "Daddy, I painted you a picture of Uncle Hazard's pinecone palace. I could hang it up on your wall for you to look at when you wake up."

"The dog is out in the car with Grandma Horace and Uncle Buddy," Becksie explains.

"Yeah, out in the car," says Jitters.

Caroline says, "Daddy, are you ever gonna wake up?" and Cyrus says, "Yeah, are you, Daddy?"

I lean in close to him and whisper in his ear. "Daddy, me and Gentle are here beside you too. We went to see Livy One today, her grave. And Mama wants me to sing for you cause the new baby is coming soon, and we might not get to visit so much. I sure hope it wakes you up, because don't you think you've been sleeping long enough? Hey, I meant to tell you that I've been reading some Emily Dickinson and e.e. cummings.

They're fine poets, Daddy, and I also been reading Willa Cather too. She wrote a fine book about a girl who loved to sing just like me."

Gentle whispers, "Daddy, I love you!" and she touches his face with her fingers, and gives him butterfly kisses.

Before I start singing, Emmett leans down close to Daddy and says, "Daddy, Uncle Buddy has an iguana named Pearl. She looks like a miniature dinosaur, I swear. Daddy, if you can hear me, I'm sorry, real sorry. Now Livy Two is going to sing something for you, Daddy." Emmett nods to me, and I start in singing the medley that Daddy missed when he didn't make it to the Mountain Dance and Folk Music Festival. I don't have my guitar, but I sing all the songs I know by heart.

Mathew the Mennonite drives a black truck.
He shapes our beds out of trees from the piney woods
and wears a preacher's calling hat.
Mathew the Mennonite drives a black truck.

Uncle Hazard and Emmett, they went fishing.
They caught trout and catfish and a walleye.
They fired up the fire and they ate for days.
On wheelbarrow canvas

Louise painted her some peacocks
and rubbed in raspberries and rose petals for clouds.
She smeared in dandelion heart
to give the sky a sun.
Louise painted her some peacocks.

Then I sing the song about Daddy I couldn't sing before when the words were stuck in my throat after the accident, and everyone sings it with me.

Daddy's eyes flash pure joy
and I can picture him as a boy.
When he gets an idea in his head
Daddy swings me 'round the holler
even though I'm growing taller
and I listen to all the words he's said.
He said, "Sing something pretty for the folks."
He said, "They need to hear your pretty voice."
He said, "Sing something pretty to fill our
*   hearts with peace."*
He said, "Lord, I got me a fine passel of young'uns."

Then something happens. Maybe it's Livy One beating her bright angel fairy wings over the bed, or maybe Daddy just hears us singing to him. I don't know what. But I do know that I see it. While we're all singing, Daddy's hand moves. It moves just the tiniest bit, but I see his fingers squeeze Gentle's hand. Mama sees it too, and I watch her take a breath. Daddy doesn't open his eyes, and he doesn't sit up or anything. He just holds Gentle's hand. A tiny squeeze. That's all, and that's enough. Daddy's listening. Maybe one day he'll come home.

ACKNOWLEDGMENTS

I would like to thank my editor, Melanie Cecka, for helping me find the heart of this manuscript and believing in this family, and Catherine Frank, Janet Pascal, and Margaret Cahoon for their most thoughtful edits during the final revisions. I would also like to thank my agent, Marianne Merola, who, after reading an early draft, said, "The kid's blind, the dad's in trouble, and they're broke. How about a little hope here?" I am grateful to Ellen Slezak, whose generous edits helped me shape the final drafts. I also must thank my son, Flannery, who wasn't afraid to write "cheesy" in the margins when it was, and I thank my daughter, Lucy, who loved each draft from the beginning and my daughter, Norah, who demanded more Uncle Hazard stories from her car seat. I want to thank my parents who babysat for me during the final attack of copy-edits and allowed me blissful time to concentrate. I want to thank George Hagen, whose insightful notes made me trust what I was doing. I am so blessed by my friendship with Craig Gillespie, who brought Uncle Hazard and his pinecone palace to life in beautiful paintings that brighten our home every day. I would also like to thank Alice McDermott, Heather Dundas, Diana Wagman, and Terri Seligman for their support and friendship.

Many thanks to Monica Benalcazar for her beautiful design for the jacket image, and Kelley McIntyre, who designed the inside of the book. I would like to thank the Author's Guild and the Society of Children's Books Writers and Illustrators for their help and support, and SCBWI, too, for establishing programs like Writer's Day.

I am deeply indebted to the music and words of Loretta Lynn, Patsy Cline, Lucinda Williams, Hank Williams, Earl Scruggs, Tom Waits, Steve Earle, Mississippi John Hurt, Alison Kraus, Gillian Welch, Iris Dement, Karen Carpenter, The Cox Family, Willie Nelson, Dolly Parton, Michelle Shocked, Robert Johnson, k.d. lang, T Bone Burnett, Reno & Smiley and the Tennessee Cut-Ups, Bascom Lamar Lunsford, Jim Lunsford, and his lovely singing daughters, Nancy, Tomi, and Teresa, as all of their songs and stories offered me solace and hope in my car, driving kids around as I tried to find the voice of a child songwriter in Livy Two Weems. I want to thanks Bernadette Murphy for her advice regarding Mama's knitting wool.

I would very much like to express my appreciation to the Braille Institute of Southern California's Library Services and Universal Media Services staff members, especially Julie Uyeno for her wonderful tour of the facility and the history of the Braille Institute; Marvin Bennett for explaining how the Telephone Reader Program works; Liz Wilhelm for reading Dr. Seuss in Braille for me and talking about growing up blind; Rafael Camarena for showing me his graphic designs for the blind and the Braille machines; and Carol Jimenez for talking to me about the education of blind children and the great importance of learning Braille.

I would also like to thank Iris Lunsford, who talked to me at length on a hot summer day about what it was like to work at the blacksmith shop at Ghost Town in the Sky in 1961 when the park first opened in Maggie Valley. And I am grateful to Patty Pylant Kosier who sent me her book, *Maggie of Maggie Valley NC*, about her mother, for whom Maggie Valley was named.

I want to thank Paulina Jones, who read a very early, wobbly draft of *Gentle's Holler* and wrote a book report. I am also very appreciative of my high school and college years in Knoxville, Tennessee, and the many road trips to the Smoky Mountains. And finally,

I am most grateful to Cheri Peters of the Sewanee Writers Conference in Sewanee, Tennessee, and John and Elizabeth Grammar of the Sewanee Young Writers Conference, where my work was heard and nurtured for many summers. This book is for my husband, Kiffen, who told me the stories of his childhood, growing up one of thirteen children in Tennessee and North Carolina.